CW00828855

RANGERS AT BAY

RANGERS AT BAY

Bradford Scott

CHIVERS
THORNDIKE

This Large Print edition is published by BBC Audiobooks Ltd, Bath, England and by Thorndike Press®, Waterville, Maine, USA.

Published in 2004 in the U.K. by arrangement with Golden West Literary Agency.

Published in 2004 in the U.S. by arrangement with Golden West Literary Agency.

U.K. Hardcover ISBN 0–7540–6977–X (Chivers Large Print)
U.K. Softcover ISBN 0–7540–6978–8 (Camden Large Print)
U.S. Softcover ISBN 0–7862–6544–2 (Nightingale)

This book is fiction. No resemblance is intended between any character herein and any person, living or dead; any such resemblance is purely coincidental.

The text of this Large Print edition is unabridged.
Other aspects of the book may vary from the original edition.

Set in 16 pt. New Times Roman.

Printed in Great Britain on acid-free paper.

British Library Cataloguing in Publication Data available

Library of Congress Cataloging-in-Publication Data

Scott, Bradford, 1893–1975.
    Rangers at bay / Bradford Scott.
      p. cm.
    ISBN 0–7862–6544–2 (lg. print : sc : alk. paper)
    1. Texas Rangers—Fiction. 2. Texas—Fiction.
    3. Large type books. I. Title.
PS3537.C9265R36 2004
813'.54—dc22   2004043795

One

Captain Jim McNelty, the famous commander of the Border Battalion, swore a blistering oath and crumpled the newspaper in his gnarled hands. Then he carefully smoothed it out on his tabledesk.

'Here's another one.' He passed the paper to Walt Slide.

The man the Mexican *peons* of the Rio Grande river villages named *El Halcon*—The Hawk—took the sheet and read the glaring black scareheads:

OUTMODED
No Longer An Asset; A Liability
Border Depredations of the 'Texas Dangers'
May Cause International Explosion

There followed a lengthy and vitriolic article beginning, 'How long must the people of Texas put up with this archaic institution of misfits?'

Slade read it carefully to the end. He glanced at Captain Jim, the concentration furrow a bit deeper between his level black brows.

'Blaine Stewart's *Herald*,' he remarked, glancing at the heading.

'Yes. He's going stronger all the time, and

1

it'll be copied by every paper in the state,' growled Captain Jim. 'Not that I give a blankety-blank-blank about such driveling nonsense,' he added, glowering at the offending sheet.

Slade spoke gravely, 'I'm not so sure it's nonsense, sir.'

Captain Jim bristled. 'You're not, eh? Well, what do you figure it is?'

'I think,' Slade said, spacing his words deliberately, 'that it is a well-planned, organized, carefully prepared and well-financed conspiracy to do away with the Texas Rangers as a law-enforcement body. And if we don't step lively, it'll do just that.'

Captain Jim sat bolt upright in his chair. 'Walt,' he said, 'folks who know the truth are in the habit of saying that you're not only the most fearless of the rangers but also the smartest. Usually I'm ready to go along with them. But right now, I've got a feeling you're talking through your hat.'

Slade smiled, the little devils of laughter dancing in the back of his cold eyes, although he was in scant mood for mirth.

'All right,' he said. 'But don't forget what happened to the State Police, as the rangers were called during that portion of the Reconstruction years. They were disbanded by the legislature, over Governor Davis' veto. I'll admit that the State Police were hardly representative of the rangers before and after, but just the same, although a rather grubby lot, they were considered the rangers of their day. There was a strikingly similar campaign against the State Police, a singular unanimity on the part of the Press, with somebody in the background pulling the strings. That crusade, if we may call it such, was vicious, with every possible fault or mistake brought to the fore and every accomplishment and virtue minimized. Until folks in general got to believing the half-truths, the glosses and omissions; and the State Police got the boot.

'Of course,' he added, 'in less than a year the rangers were back in the saddle, reorganized and with greater prestige than ever, and have been ever since. But what happened once could happen again. There's an element in the state that could very well do without the rangers, and that element will be wholeheartedly behind the attempt. There's not an outlaw or other criminal in Texas who wouldn't rejoice if the rangers were abolished. The rangers have a record of excellence second to none, but public opinion is a fickle thing and can be played upon successfully by shrewd manipulators who have access to the printed word.'

Slade paused to roll and light a cigarette, while Captain Jim growled and snorted.

'Things are ticklish along the Border right now,' Slade resumed. 'Whenever we go after the hellions there, a howl goes up in *manana*

3

land. There are certain interests up here that have a big stake south of the Rio Grande and are very sensitive to reactions on the other side of the river. They would not be exactly brokenhearted should the rangers be disbanded. They can be counted on to give moral support, if not some of a more practical character, to Blaine Stewart and his scheme.'

'That blankety-blank Stewart!' stormed Captain Jim. 'He's at the bottom of all this trouble.'

'Perhaps,' Slade conceded soberly. 'He hates the rangers and with him it's a personal matter. Don't forget, the rangers killed his brother. By accident, yes, but Stewart has never been convinced that it was an accident. He comes of Scottish Highland stock and in his veins is the feuding blood of the glens that never forgets an injury, and never forgives.'

'His brother was killed years ago,' Captain Jim replied.

'Yes,' Slade said, 'and in my opinion he has been biding his time and nursing his revenge through the years. Working and waiting till the time was ripe for him to take vengeance for his brother's killing. He figures that time has come. Since this thing began to break, I've made it my business to do a little research on *Senor* Blaine Stewart and I've learned plenty, of a very serious nature. He's a very rich man, now. In addition to just about the biggest and best ranch in the Big Bend country and his newspaper, he owns a couple of gold mines and a quicksilver mine, and has stock in railroads and other ventures. He's been dabbling in politics, too, and has influence that reaches far beyond the confines of Brewster County. He's in a position to make trouble and if he isn't stopped, he will make it.'

Captain McNelty began to look really concerned. He had great faith in Walt Slade's judgment of men and affairs, and the earnestness with which his tall young lieutenant spoke was disquieting. He got up and paced the floor, muttering under his bristly mustache. It was clear, despite his white hair and lined face, from the swing of his stride and the spring of his step that he had far from lost the fire and activity of his youth.

Slade also stood up, sauntered to the window and gazed out. Abruptly, he turned to face his superior. Captain Jim paused in his amble, with an inquiring glance.

Although he was himself a stalwart six-footer, the ranger captain had to raise his eyes a bit to meet Slade's level gaze, and Captain Jim thought he had never seen a man with broader shoulders or a deeper chest. And Slade's face did not belie his splendid form. It was a face dominated by long gray eyes with thick black lashes; cold, reckless eyes of pale gray, that nevertheless could at times be as sunny as summer seas. A rather wide mouth, grin-quirked at the corners, relieved somewhat the sternness of the high-bridged nose and the powerful chin and jaw. His lean cheeks were deeply bronzed and his pushed back 'J.B.' revealed thick, crisp black hair.

Slade wore the homely but efficient garb of the rangeland—Levi's, scuffed half-boots of softly tanned leather, faded blue shirt with vivid neckerchief looped at the throat; and he wore it as a courtier wears velvet and samite. Around his sinewy waist were double cartridge belts, and from the carefully-worked and oiled cut-out holsters protruded the plain black butts of heavy guns, from which his slender, powerful hands never seemed to stray far.

All of which, Captain Jim took in with a single glance and an unconscious nod of approval.

'Well,' he barked, 'what the devil are we going to do about it?'

'I think,' Slade replied, 'that with your permission, sir, I'll take a little ride down to the Big Bend country where Blaine Stewart's ranch is located. Might be able to learn something. And, anyhow, a lot of things that need attention have been happening in that section of late; the Border is just a mite active.'

'You're darn right!' grunted McNelty. 'Too blasted active. Plenty of off-color shenanigans been going on down there. And a lot of it in the section where Stewart's holding is located. Wouldn't be surprised if the wind spider has something to do with it. Been yelps for "Texas

6

Dangers," as that cross between a spavined sheep and a horned toad calls us. I ought to let the ungrateful hellions stew in their own juice for a while and see how they like it. But I've a notion you've got an idea, all right. Doubt if you're very well known as a ranger down there. But how about as *El Halcon*?'

'Oh, I suppose somebody will spot me as *El Halcon* before long,' Slade replied cheerfully.

'You'll get your comeuppance some day, posing as a blasted owlhoot too smart to get caught,' fumed the captain. 'Some trigger-happy sheriff or marshal will let you have it before you can explain.'

'Nobody's had much luck so far,' Slade answered, still cheerful. The captain snorted.

'That reputation has come in handy more than once,' Slade reminded him. 'Outlaws take me to their bosom as a blood brother and sometimes do a little talking or make a slip they wouldn't make if they knew me for a ranger.'

'There's something in the Scriptures about being taken to Beelzebub's bosom and what happens because of it, and the Devil's the Devil no matter what name you call him,' grunted Captain Jim.

'It's also been said that the Devil takes care of his own,' Slade said smilingly.

'That I can believe,' Captain Jim declared heartily. 'Well, go ahead and get shot, if it makes you happy. Sometime I'm going to

7

crack down on you and order you to stop it. See if I don't.'

Slade grinned, for he didn't believe Captain Jim would do any such thing, although there was no doubt that he worried over the reputation Slade had built up from operating undercover whenever possible. *El Halcon*! The singingest man in the Southwest, and with the fastest gunhand!

Slade picked up the copy of the *Herald* again. 'They're employing exactly the same tactics as were used against the State Police,' he said. 'Listen to this passage. I'm willing to bet a hatful of pesos that it was taken, word for word, from old newspaper files of that period.'

While Captain Jim snorted and pulled his mustache, he read:

'We had a chance to look over this particular band that has more than once invoked *la ley de fuga*—killing a prisoner while attempting to "escape," especially against harmless Mexicans or small landholders, humble people with no one to champion them.

'Yes, we looked them over. They were well-filled with good old copper distilled, and they had a coppery appearance about the nose, and a watery look out of the eyes, and were men of exceeding great stature, two of them laid end to end would have measured all of nine feet.

8

'And they were of the cavalry breed, mounted on the ribs of sway-backed, double-barreled mustangs of an extremely fine stock—so fine that they hardly cast a shadow; whose hip bones did protrude mightily, whereon these valiant warriors were wont to hang their massive felt helmets when they sought their pillows at night. They—'

'That's enough!' bawled Captain Jim, his mustache bristling in his scarlet face. 'I don't want to hear any more of that guff! The blankety-blanked, snake-blooded vinegaroon! Who'd pay any attention to such tommyrot!'

Slade shook with laughter. 'It's pretty strong, all right,' he conceded. Almost instantly he was grave again.

'I know it sounds like plain tommyrot,' he said, 'but don't underestimate it. There is no blast so powerful, so withering, as the blast of ridicule. At first, people laugh, then they get to thinking and before they realize it, they are accepting it as gospel truth. The result, aroused public opinion that doesn't know what it's aroused about, but is out to crack any head in sight. We can snap our fingers at it and liken it to the crackling of thorns under a pot, but we mustn't ignore it, hoping it will go away. We've got to fight back.

'And,' he added grimly, 'that's just what we're going to do. I'm going after the big he-wolf of the pack himself—Blaine Stewart. I've a notion that somewhere he's vulnerable, that somewhere there's a chink in his armor. I aim to find out about that and take advantage of it.'

Looking at his lieutenant's eyes that were now the color of snow-dusted ice under a stormy sky, Captain Jim began to feel better. And he reflected that he would not be in Blaine Stewart's shoes for all Blaine Stewart's money, power and prestige. He'd seen that look in Walt Slade's eyes before—the terrible eyes of *El Halcon*—and, tough old frontiersman that he was, had shivered a little over what came of it. He drew a deep breath.

'When you going to start?' he asked.

'I think I'll take the night train to Marfa, if you can arrange for a stock car to be hooked on for the accommodation of my horse,' Slade replied. 'I can make it to Marfa by around noon, and from there I'll ride south until I'm in the vicinity of *Senor* Stewart's stamping ground. After that, what I do will depend on how events shape up. Perhaps I'll get a lucky break of some kind. I want to contact Stewart and have a chance to study him and perhaps learn things I don't know about him. It's rugged country down there and it always has been lawless. A man born and brought up in that section may have something in his past he'd rather not have investigated too closely. Maybe I'll have a chance to get him where the

10

hair's short. A man in his position sometimes can't afford to have old happenings dug up, especially when he's in the public eye as Stewart is right now.'

'Sounds like sense to me,' grunted Captain Jim. 'Okay, I'll fix it for the cayuse; you wouldn't be yourself if you didn't have Shadow along. Sometimes I think it's him who really works things out, not you.'

'He does his share,' Slade smiled.

Captain Jim was as good as his word and the following afternoon found Walt Slade riding south from Marfa on a trail that he knew would lead him to the wide, mountain-locked valley which was his destination.

Two

The dead man lay in the middle of the trail, his glazed, unseeing eyes glaring up at the evening sky. His arms were wide-flung, his legs stuck out straight and stiff. His close-cropped brown hair bristled up from his scalp. His cadaverous face, upon which rested an unnatural pallor, was contorted in a look of horror and surprise that was frozen by the cold hand of death into a changeless photo of his last living expression. A dark blotch, smudged with black-edged brown, stained the front of his faded blue shirt.

A few yards from where he lay, the trail to

11

the north bent sharply between encroaching walls of high brush. Sloping up, it ended in a knife edge that gave the impression of a sheer drop beyond, but which was really the steep incline of the far side of the ridge it topped a short distance from where he lay. The sharply-drawn edge of the lip was clear against the deepening blue of the northern sky, glowing in a ray of sunlight from the west.

The sudden appearance of the dimpled crown of a broad-brimmed, well-worn 'J.B.' above the edge seemed a natural and predestined occurrence.

The hat rose higher to reveal Walt Slade's bronzed face; then the sleek, lean head, the graceful neck, sinewy withers and mighty barrel that swelled upward into breath-catching completeness as Shadow, his splendid black horse, topped the ridge.

Slade glanced down the trail. His hand tightened on the split reins and his voice rang out.

'Hold it!'

The black horse froze and made a striking picture against the blue background of the sky, ears pricked forward, eyes fixed on the motionless form lying in the dust of the trail.

Slade gave the body a single swift glance; then his gaze minutely searched every foot of the growth hemming the trail, centered for an instant on the bend ahead that abruptly cut off his view to the south. For a moment he studied the movements of a couple of birds fluttering from limb to limb on a nearby bush, chirping contentedly. Satisfied with his surroundings and convinced that nothing but the birds and the beasts which belonged there were holed up in the chaparral, he lowered his gaze to the dead man once more. Dismounting lithely, he strode forward, his movement a rhythmical perfection, and squatted on his heels beside the body. He studied the dead face a moment, then stretched out a hand and touched the blood-soaked shirt front.

'Not dead long, Shadow,' he told the horse. 'The blood has hardly begun to stiffen.'

The brown smudge blending with the darker bloodstain interested him; he studied its darkened edges.

'Powder burns, feller,' he said. 'Must have shoved the gun right into his ribs.'

With deft fingers he opened the dead man's shirt and stared at the wound in his chest, his black brows drawing together. Then he gently turned the body over on its face. The back of the shirt was unmarred by rent or tear. He turned the body back to gaze again at the bullet wound.

'That's funny,' he remarked aloud. 'The look of a heavy calibre bullet—maybe a .45— but the slug didn't go through.'

His eyes dark with thought, he stood erect and studied the ground nearby, walking several yards down the trail. He glanced at the flanking growth, scrutinized it narrowly, shook his black head and stared at the ground once more. Squatting comfortably and rocking back on his heels, he fished the makin's from a shirt pocket and began to roll a cigarette with the slim fingers of his left hand, gazing at the dark tangle of brush all the while.

Abruptly the tiny rectangle of white paper fluttered to the ground. Slade straightened up with a movement of lithe grace and stood gazing down the trail to the south, the thumbs of his slender hands hooked over the black butts of the guns flaring out from his sinewy hips. From beyond the bend in the trail sounded a swift, rhythmic clicking.

The clicking grew louder, resolved to the steady beat of approaching horses' hoofs. An instant later, two horsemen raced around the bend going at top speed. At the sight of *El Halcon*, they jerked their mounts to a skating halt, their right hands flashing down.

With fingers coiled around the butts of the guns at their hips they froze grotesquely, straining forward, eyes dilating. Slade's hands had moved in a swift blur of action and the black muzzles, rock-steady, of the two long guns yawned at the pair.

Slade spoke, his voice drawling, musical, but holding a note that was not to be disregarded.

'Better not,' he said. 'That is, unless you'd feel more comfortable where this gent is, instead of where you are.'

14

The newcomers, tall, broad-shouldered men as lithe and sinewy as panthers, glared at him. The taller of the two was exceedingly handsome, his features almost cameo-like in their regularity, his hair crisply golden and inclined to curl, his eyes a deep blue, his mouth thin-lipped and hard but finely shaped. The other was less outstanding, but he bore a resemblance that was unmistakable. Brothers, Slade concluded.

The tall man spoke, his voice harsh with anger.

'Feller, you can't get away with it,' he said. 'You got the drop on us, all right, and I reckon you can do us in the same as you did poor Tom Hargus, if you're of a mind to. But you can't get away with it; the Hargus boys will hunt you down if they have to cover every inch of Texas.'

Slade regarded the speaker speculatively for a moment. Abruptly, he motioned with his left-hand gun.

'Unfork with your hands up,' he ordered. 'Move, both of you.'

The pair obeyed, glaring and muttering, sliding awkwardly from their hulls to stand stiff and resentful a half-dozen paces distant.

Slade gestured to the taller man. 'Come here.'

The man obeyed sullenly, his hands shoulder-high. Slade flipped one gun in his hand and extended it to the other, butt foremost.

15

'Take it and look it over,' he directed. 'Be careful how you handle it—the other one is right where you first saw it.'

The man, a bewildered look on his face, instinctively glanced at *El Halcon*'s left-hand gun. He saw that the hammer was at full cock, the trigger pulled back, with only the weight of Slade's thumb hooked over the milled tip to prevent the firing pin from falling onto the cartridge. He lowered his right hand slowly and gingerly reached for the proffered Colt.

'Look it over carefully,' Slade repeated. 'See if it's been fired recently.'

The man obeyed. 'No, it hasn't,' he admitted sullenly. Slade shot the second man a glance.

'Do you take his word for it or do you wish to look for yourself?' he asked.

'What Cart says is good enough for me,' the other grunted.

'Okay,' Slade said. 'Hand it back, carefully,' he told the man in front of him. 'All right, here's the other one.'

The man, Cart, took the other Colt, his attitude changing. He seemed to forget the gun Slade held, which was trained on his heart. His companion took a step forward to peer over his shoulder.

Cart grinned; a thin grin that showed teeth almost as white and even as Slade's own. Hardly glancing at the gun, he held it out, butt first.

16

'Feller,' he said, 'I reckon it's up to Wes and me to eat a mite of crow. Nope, neither of these irons has been shot recent, and I'm ready to testify to it in court, if necessary. But you can't hold it against us for jumping at conclusions like we did. It did look funny, you'll have to admit. I'm Cart Mason and this is my brother, Wes. No, I don't want to look at your saddle gun, I've seen enough to satisfy me. I didn't catch your handle?'

Slade supplied it and the brothers nodded gravely as Slade began manufacturing another cigarette.

'Who is that fellow?' Slade asked, gesturing to the body.

'Tom Hargus, the youngest of the Hargus brothers,' Cart Mason replied. 'There's two more of 'em—Hank and Andy. Tom just got out of jail.'

'What was he in jail for?' Slade asked.

'Old Blaine Stewart had him locked up for slick-ironin',' Cart replied. 'He did nine months on a year's sentence.'

Slade's eyes narrowed. 'Time off for good behavior,' he translated. 'Guilty?'

Cart Mason shrugged his broad shoulders. 'Well, the jury must have thought so,' he replied evasively. 'Judge Parker appeared sort of doubtful; anyhow, he gave Tom the minimum.'

Slade nodded thoughtfully. 'Wasn't caught dead to rights, then,' he commented.

'Nope,' Mason replied. 'Blaine Stewart's range boss, Joe Callison, ran onto a scorched calf, stomped out the fire and saw Hargus riding away from there. He chased him and got winged, but he creased Hargus and brought him in. Stewart and the Harguses had had disagreements already and Stewart pushed the charge. Hargus swore that he was just taking a short cut across the corner of Stewart's Forked S range to the Hargus' Bradded H ranchhouse. Stewart came back that he'd given the Harguses orders to keep off his holding, and that Hargus had no business trespassing in the first place. I've a notion that sort of influenced the jury. Besides, Stewart is the biggest owner in the section and has plenty of dinero and plenty of political pull, and he's an oldtimer here while the Harguses are sort of newcomers. Guess that influenced the jury, too. Anyhow they brought in a guilty verdict and Tom went to jail swearing he'd even up with Stewart soon as he got out. Looks like he might have tried it with Stewart, or one of his bunch, and come off second best.'

'Came off second best with somebody, all right,' agreed Slade, who had been listening to Mason's story with lively interest. 'Wonder what became of his horse?'

Mason glanced at the wall of growth. 'Reckon it cut through the brush after pitching him,' he said. 'You didn't hear any shots?'

'I was on the other side of the ridge,' Slade

18

replied. 'Judging from the appearance of the bloodstain, Hargus was plugged some time back. The sound of a gun wouldn't carry far over the hill.'

The Masons nodded. 'We didn't hear anything, either,' said Cart. 'But I reckon we must have been three or four miles down the trail when it happened, and the brush is thick and would hold back the sound. We were headed for Marfa—railroad town but I reckon we'd better pack what's left of poor Tom back to Alforki; we can put off our trip till tomorrow. Wes has a new hull waiting at the express office and we figured to pick it up and have a night in town.'

Slade's glance automatically rested on the Masons' saddles, and abruptly his black brows drew together thoughtfully, his gaze fixing on the horn of Wes' tree; it showed a ragged tear. His all-embracing glance noted that a rifle was snugged in the saddle boot of one rig; the other rig's boot was empty.

Wes Mason contemplated the body of Hargus. 'My horse will pack double,' he said. 'Reckon we can tie him on back of the saddle. If you fellers will give me a hand—'

He approached Hargus' heavy form doubtfully, but Slade picked up the body as if it had been that of a child and gently draped it across the horse's flanks back of the cantle. Cart Mason shook his head admiringly.

'Wouldn't want to have a tussle with you,

Slade,' he said. 'I've a notion you don't know how strong you are.'

When the body was securely lashed in place they mounted their horses and rode down the trail. Slade replied to occasional remarks by the Masons, but his attention was on the ground over which they passed, though in a manner that was not noticeable to his companions.

The evening had turned sultry and the reddish beams of the low-lying sun were fierce. Slade loosened the neckerchief looped about his throat. Cart Mason shucked off his coat and draped it across his horse's withers. Wes, however, retained his despite the heat.

The trail dipped into a wide hollow, writhed up a long slope and topped a second rise; abruptly the country below lay before them like a map.

'There's Alforki Valley,' observed Cart Mason. 'All the northwest end—except our little holding, the Bar M—is Blaine Stewart's range. The Hargus spread, that they bought from old Conrad Withrow, is down nearest to the south hills, something folks have talked about of late.'

He did not amplify the cryptic remark, but the insinuation was plain to Slade, who asked no questions. He ran his eye over the great valley. It was excellent rangeland.

It was not hard to understand how the valley came by its peculiar name. *Alforki*, Slade knew, was a Spanish word that designated the wide canvas or leather bags, one on either side of a packsaddle, hanging from the crosses on the saddle's top. The valley was roughly the shape of the twin bags fanned out from the saddle. It was wide and bulging at either end, narrowing curiously in the middle. Rather, though, it was the shape of lop-sided packs, for it was much wider to the north, where the eastern hills, stepping up quickly to mountains, were misty with distance. The hills to the north rolled up high and broad. Those to the south were even higher, but in contrast, the northern elevations were rugged and irregular, featured by frowning cliffs, jagged peaks and dark canyon mouths.

Cart Mason noted Slade's embracing glance.

'There are straight shoots to Mexico, for those that know them, through those hills to the south,' he commented. 'Wideloopers, in the old days, knew all those cracks and holes. There are folks, especially those who've lost cows, who say they're a mite too well known even in these days,' he added grimly.

'Widelooping still going on hereabouts?' Slade asked.

'We have lost considerable head, and so have other folks, particularly Blaine Stewart, whose Slash S has been catching blazes of late,' Mason replied. 'Looks like a south of the Border outfit is working the section overtime, at least so I figure. There are folks hereabouts who think different.'

Slade nodded and continued to survey the great valley. Not far from the lower slope of the hills they had been traversing, he saw a cluster of buildings that looked like doll houses in the distance.

'That's Alforki down there,' said Cart Mason. 'Reckon we'd better pack Tom into town and turn him over to the sheriff. Barnes can notify his brothers.'

Slade offered no objections, so they rode down the winding trail to the base of the hills. An hour later found them passing between a straggle of buildings that lined the crooked main street of the town. These gradually gave way to more imposing edifices. Cart Mason gestured to a solid-looking brick building that sat apart.

'That's the *Herald* Building, where Blaine Stewart publishes his newspaper,' he said. 'Got a big circulation all over the state. Stewart sees to it that it gets to folks who sell newspapers everywhere. Or rather, Hodson Vane, who's the editor and runs the shebang for Stewart, sees to it. A mighty smart feller, Vane. Gets along well with folks, too. Right next door is the bank. Reckon Stewart just about owns that, too. Reckon he'll end up owning the whole county, the way he's going.'

'Must be quite a gent,' Slade remarked.

'He is,' said Mason. 'Wait till you see him—

betcha you'll think so, all right.'

Slade already thought so, but he did not see fit to enlighten Cart Mason.

Shortly after passing the *Herald* Building Mason pulled to a halt before a squat structure with barred windows.

'Here's where the sheriff has his office when he's here, and he's here most of the time, a lot more than he is at the county seat,' observed Mason. 'Used to be just a deputy stationed here, but now Barnes, himself, is usually around. We'll pack Tom in.'

Slade lifted the body from the horse's back and they entered the office.

Sheriff Dave Barnes, a bulky oldtimer with faded but alert blue eyes, sunken chops and a drooping mustache, came to his feet with a rush as they entered.

'What in blazes?' he demanded.

Cart Mason related what had happened, so far as he knew. The sheriff wagged his head, shot a keen glance at Slade and spoke.

'Lay him on the bunk over there and cover him with a blanket,' he directed. 'Cart, get one from the cells in back. Andy Hargus is in town right now—over to the Four Deuces saloon. Go get him, Wes; we'll wait here till you come back.'

Slade deposited Tom Hargus' body on the bunk, while Cart Mason procured a blanket and draped it over the stark form. Wes Mason hurried out to fetch Hargus' brother.

'You say he was laying in the trail when you rode over the lip?' the sheriff asked of Slade.

'That's right,' the ranger replied.

'Dead when you came up to him?'

Slade nodded. 'Been dead for a while, I figure. Not overly long, though; the blood on his shirt hadn't begun to stiffen yet.'

The sheriff nodded and tugged his mustache. 'Going to be the devil over this,' he predicted. 'The Harguses will blame Blaine Stewart, sure as blazes. I've got to get hold of Stewart in a hurry. Where you from, feller?' he shot at Slade.

'Rode down from the north,' *El Halcon* replied easily. 'Was busy over around Laredo, last.'

Which was perfectly true, although Slade did not, choose to go into detail concerning his activities around the Border town.

The sheriff frowned, seemed about to ask further questions. Before he could speak, however, the doorway was filled by a man who hurried in from the deepening darkness of the street. Behind him tagged Wes Mason.

The newcomer paused, glaring about with hot blue eyes. He had a massive jaw, a great beak of a nose, a jutting chin and tawny hair that bristled from beneath his battered 'J.B.' He was quite good looking in a rugged sort of way.

'Barnes, what happened to Tom?' he demanded harshly.

24

'Looks like he had some bad luck, Andy,' the sheriff replied, gesturing to the draped form on the bunk.

Andy Hargus crossed the room with a slow, ponderous tread. He drew back the blanket and gazed down into his brother's dead face. And as he did so, his own comely features settled into an expression of terrible hatred. He replaced the blanket and straightened up, tall almost as Walt Slade, and broader. He fixed the silent group with his burning eyes.

'So they finally did for the poor kid, eh?' he rumbled. 'Not enough to have him locked up on a phoney charge, they have to do him in.'

'Easy, Andy,' the sheriff admonished. 'You don't know who did for Tom any more than the rest of us do.'

'I can answer with one guess,' growled the giant, striding forward and pounding the sheriff's desk with a hamlike fist. 'Barnes, either you do something about it or I will. I listened to you when they pulled that cold deck on the kid last year, and what did it get me? "Let the law take its course," you said, and Tom went to jail. This time I figure to do my own lawin'.'

The sheriff was about to answer when steps sounded outside. Two men entered the room. The foremost was a blocky old man with grizzled hair; smoking a cigar. His square, close-cropped head, his large features, his alert eyes were those of a fighter. The other was a

25

lanky individual with keen, shifty eyes that covered the room in one swift glance.

Andy Hargus let out a bellow of rage. 'Stewart, you sneaking, fanging, drygulching sidewinder!' he howled. He jerked his gun from its sheath and lined sights with the old man's broad breast.

Three

Walt Slade moved like a flash of light. His slender fingers wrapped around Hargus' wrist like rods of steel and wrenched his hand up even as the gun boomed. The bullet whined over the old man's head and buried itself in the wall. The lanky man jerked a gun and fired; the slug fanned Slade's face as he and Hargus went sideways. He ground the bones of Hargus' wrist together with intolerable force. Hargus yelled with pain and dropped his gun. He whirled and clinched with his opponent. Back and forth they reeled in a mighty wrestling grip.

They crashed into the sheriff's desk. Over it went, the sheriff and the wreckage of his splintered chair beneath it. Another chair went to matchwood under their boots. The giant bellowed with fury and put forth his strength, nearly swinging Slade from his feet. They caromed into a bench upon which stood a bucket of water. Over went the pail, the spilled water sloshing under their boots. Slade slipped on the wet boards and the other's great weight forced him to one knee. Even as he went down he shifted his grip to the giant's bulging forearms. A mighty heave, a tensing of his great muscles, and Andy Hargus flew over his head and through the air to hit the floor with a crash that shook the building.

Before he could get to his feet Slade was on top of him, one knee grinding into the small of his back, levering his arm up between his shoulder blades till Hargus bawled with pain.

'Get the other one!' Slade shouted to the sheriff, who was scrambling from beneath the smashed desk, screeching curses.

The lanky man was dancing about, trying to get in another shot. He leaped forward, his gun throwing down; but the sheriff hit him squarely in the chest with the point of his shoulder. Under the shock of the impact both men lost their footing and thudded to the floor, the lanky man's gun clattering across the room.

The sheriff came to his feet like a cat, a gun in each hand.

'Get out of here, Stewart!' he bellowed. 'Get out of here, and take that loco Callison with you! Get out, I say!'

The old man removed the cigar from his mouth and blew a cloud of smoke. He glanced about as coolly as if he had been watching the rehearsing of an act.

'Okay, Barnes,' he said. 'Come on, Joe, let's get going.' He turned to where Slade held Andy Hargus helpless. 'Much obliged,' he said, and vanished into the night. The lanky man lurched to his feet, picked up his gun and holstered it. He cast a look of venomous hatred at the prostrate Hargus and obediently followed Stewart out the door.

Slade let go of Andy Hargus' wrist, straightened up and stepped back warily. The giant got to his feet and stood rubbing his strained arm and glowering at Slade. Suddenly, however, a grin split his craggy features, revealing crooked but very white teeth.

'Didn't believe there was a man in Texas who could do it,' he rumbled. 'No hard feelings, feller, even if you did keep me from plugging that sidewinder.'

'I've a notion you would be sorry about it now if you had,' Slade returned gravely. 'Unless he had it hid somewhere, he wasn't packing a gun. It would have been mighty like a cold-blooded killing.'

'You're darned right it would,' put in the sheriff. 'Andy, this big gent is due a "much obliged" from you also. You'd find yourself on a mighty tough spot about now, if it wasn't for him.'

'There oughtn't to be a law against killing a snake—with fangs or without,' growled Hargus. 'You'll notice, Barnes, that snake-eyed range boss of his was packing plenty of iron and didn't hesitate to use it.'

The Masons had taken no part in the shindig, but had kept back against the wall out of the range of flying lead. Now Cart spoke up.

'The sheriff's right, Andy,' he said. 'You put yourself on a spot. If Tom hadn't taken that shot at Joe Callison last year, maybe things would have gone different with him.'

'Tom said Callison reached first,' retorted Hargus.

'That may be. I wouldn't be surprised if it was so, but the jury didn't see it that way,' Mason pointed out. 'And the question was brought up, why should Tom have winged Callison if he wasn't up to something off-color. I'm not trying to make a case for Callison— sometimes I think Stewart is making a mistake by keeping him on and always taking up for him. But Stewart is that way; when he hates, he hates. But he's loyal to folks he considers his friends no matter what they do or who they associate with. As I said, I'm not taking up for Callison or trying to make a case for him; I'm just stating things as they stood. Right now, if you'd plugged Stewart you wouldn't have a leg to stand on, and you know it as well as I do. Use your head, feller, Wes and I are your friends, and you know we wouldn't advise anything that isn't for your good. I only wish, for the good of everybody, that you and Stewart could get together, thrash things out and maybe think better of each other. I reckon that's too much to expect, but please don't always go bustin' your cinch without thinking what it may mean for you and all the rest of us. This sort of feud is bad for everybody in the section.'

Hargus, evidently impressed, subsided into wordless rumblings.

'But just the same I'll always believe Joe Callison singed the calf and set that iron in the fire just to frame Tom,' was his final shot.

'And Blaine Stewart has always believed the rangers deliberately killed *his* brother years ago, and look at the row it's got him into,' retorted Mason. 'Oh, come on, let's go over to the Four Deuces and have a drink; I figure we all need one. Come along with us, Slade?'

El Halcon was about to accept the invitation when Sheriff Barnes spoke.

'I'd like to have a word with you first, Slade, if you don't mind,' he said. 'You can join the boys later if you want to.'

Slade nodded agreement. Hargus and the Masons left the room.

Sheriff Barnes gestured to the one remaining chair that boasted four legs. He perched himself on the corner of his sagging desk. For a long moment he eyed Slade in silence.

'Guess we can have a talk in peace and quiet, now that hot-headed young hellion's gone,' he remarked at length. 'You look to be a sensible feller; maybe you can help me get to the bottom of this mess. You say you didn't hear the shot that did Tom in?'

Slade shook his head. 'I must have been down the other side of the sag quite a way when it was fired,' he pointed out. 'Besides, it was fired some distance from where I found Hargus' body.'

The sheriff stared at him. 'By the way,' he asked, 'what became of Tom's horse?'

'Funny about that horse,' Slade answered. 'Hargus left his horse quite a way down the trail from where I found his body.'

'How do you know that?' the sheriff asked sharply.

'Because,' Slade replied, 'he came up the trail nearly half a mile on foot. I spotted his boot marks in the dust. They weren't very plain, but they could be seen, if you looked close enough.'

The sheriff tugged his mustache and frowned.

'Looked like there was a running fight for that half-mile,' Slade said.

'How's that?'

'Because I spotted something else in the dust besides boot tracks. Twice, as we rode down the sag, I saw empty rifle shells.'

'Hargus didn't have a rifle when you found him?'

'He didn't have a gun of any kind; not in sight, anyhow,' Slade replied.

'What in blazes became of the rifle if it was

him did the shooting with it?'

'That's a puzzler,' Slade admitted.

'Maybe the rifle belonged to the hellion who plugged Tom,' the sheriff hazarded. Slade slowly shook his black head.

'He wasn't shot with a rifle,' he stated conclusively.

'How do you know?'

'If you look close, you'll see that his shirt front is marked by powder bums, and the slug is still inside him. If a rifle had been held that close to his breast the bullet would have gone through him like a darning needle through a pat of butter. He was shot at close range, by a heavy-calibre gun with a mighty short barrel.'

Sheriff Barnes crossed the room to the corpse and drew back the blanket. He peered closely at the discolored shirt front, opened it and stared at the wound.

'Guess we'd better have an autopsy performed,' he said. 'I'll notify Doc Cooper, he's the coroner and will want to hold an inquest.'

'A good notion,' Slade agreed. 'You say the doctor's name is Cooper?'

'That's right,' nodded the sheriff. 'His office is just the other side of the *Herald* Building; you won't have any trouble locating it. The inquest will be held there and you should be present. Aim to coil your twine here for a spell?'

'If I can tie onto a chore of riding,' Slade

answered. 'A man has to eat.'

'So I've been told,' conceded the sheriff, smiling a little. 'Well, you shouldn't have any trouble tieing onto a job with Blaine Stewart, after saving his ornery hide from getting an airhole in it like you did. He's always on the lookout for tophands. Sometimes has trouble keeping them because of his range boss, Joe Callison. Callison is a cantankerous cuss and don't get along over well with folks. A first-rate cowman, though, and Stewart swears by him. He's stubborn as a blue-nosed mule about things like that.

'But to get back to Tom's killing. This isn't finished,' he continued gloomily. 'Andy Hargus is dead-for-sure-certain Stewart is back of the killing, and if he gets likkered up he's liable to be uglier than usual. I reckon Stewart, with Joe Callison riding herd on him, can take care of himself, maybe. Andy Hargus is a cold proposition and salty as they make 'em. I was plumb surprised by the way you handled him. Wouldn't have thought it possible, even by a gent as big as you.'

'Reckon I sort of caught him off balance,' Slade said.

'So I noticed,' the sheriff agreed dryly. 'Only I sort of had a notion it was you who were off-balance when you pitched Andy on his head. Yes, there's liable to be trouble. Joe Callison hates the Harguses as bad as they hate him and Stewart. Tom Hargus mighty nigh crippled

33

him with a slug through his shoulder last year. Callison is the sort that never forgets and never forgives. I've a notion he's got a fair dash of Indian blood. He acts it. Always been a square-shooter, so far as anybody knows, but he sure knows how to hate.'

The sheriff paused to stuff his pipe with tobacco. Slade rolled a cigarette.

'Yes, he can hate, but at that game he hasn't got anything on Stewart; *he* knows how to hate, too. He's Black Scotch by descent and they're as bad as the Indians when it comes to holding a grudge and evening it up when they get a chance. Take Stewart's row with the rangers—you may have heard something about it. It's been a lot of years since the rangers killed his brother Jeff, long before your time and I reckon you never heard about that. A troop of rangers were on the trail of a bunch of wideloopers. The rustlers had scattered into the brush and they were trying to root them out. Jeff Stewart rode out of the brush right in front of the troop, from his and Blaine's holding—wasn't anything like as big then as it is now. The rangers called on him to halt, but there were a lot of outlaw bands sashaying around in this section then, and I reckon Jeff thought that's what he was up against. Any-how he tried to hightail. One of the rangers fired a shot. He swore it was just a warning shot over Jeff's head, to make him stop, but his horse stumbled just as he pulled

34

trigger and jerked the muzzle of his rifle down. The slug drilled Jeff Stewart through the head. The court accepted the ranger's explanation, but Blaine Stewart didn't. He believed the rangers murdered his brother and nobody could convince him different.

'And here's where the Stewart hate comes in. Blaine bided his time. He could wait with his hate, just as he could wait for other things that made him a big man and a rich man. Reckon patience is a sort of keynote to his character—patience and hate. He waited, and planned. And now he's out to bust up the rangers, and a lot of folks will tell you he can do it. As to that, I don't know. But I don't agree with him. Texas needs the rangers, and aside from a short time when they were known as the State Police and were a bit fumbly, they've had a mighty good record.

'That doesn't mean a thing to Stewart. All he can think of is his hate and he's sure working it overtime. Maybe he can bust up the rangers if he isn't stopped somehow. The newspaper he owns, the *Herald*, has a big circulation, and a lot of other papers have sort of fallen in line. Stewart is rich and has a lot of influence and maybe he's sort of put the screws on other publishers. And politicians are a sensitive lot when it comes to public opinion and easy to stampede into doing something they may feel inside of them isn't just the right thing to do. So it's hard to figure just what

Stewart can or can't put over.

'A funny thing about Stewart; a more honest man never lived. And when he's got a notion he's right about something, all Hades won't stop him. You can be sure he believed Tom Hargus was widelooping his cows. He figured Hargus had violated the law, and acted accordingly. I reckon he'd have done the same thing if Hargus had been his own son.'

'Do you believe Hargus was guilty?' Slade asked.

The sheriff tugged his mustache and looked thoughtful. 'To tell the truth, I don't know what to say,' he admitted. 'Hargus was always a wild sort, but he'd never been in any trouble before. If it wasn't for—'

The sheriff hesitated, then put his thoughts into words.

'If it wasn't for his gambling, I'd say no, sure for certain,' he went on. 'Tom Hargus never could let cards alone, and he was the sort that always lost. I happen to know that before he was sent up on that slick-iron charge, he'd gotten pretty bad in debt because of poker losses. Maybe he was trying to figure a way to get out.

'Joe Callison swore he'd gotten a tip that the Harguses were slick-ironing Slash S cows and he was keeping a watch. When he spotted that tromped-out fire and the new-branded calf and then saw Tom Hargus riding along not far off, he was sure Hargus had branded that calf

36

and proceeded to accuse him of it.

'Anyhow, it was just about that time the spreads in this section began losing cows—and they been losing them ever since. Personally I figure it is a south of the Border outfit working this valley—a big outfit with plenty of savvy.'

'What makes you think that?'

'Well, the cows have to go somewhere and Mexico is about the only place they can go to find a ready market for wet beef. That is what makes some folks hereabouts suspicious of the Harguses. Their spread runs right alongside the south hills and it would be almighty easy to slide rustled cows through the canyons and passes if you happen to know 'em well enough. Stewart's holding butts right onto the Hargus spread—the Bradded H. Stewart owns the whole northwest half of the valley except for the Masons' Bar H, which the Masons bought from old Harry Arnold about a year back. Arnold was one of the real old-timers here and wouldn't sell out to Stewart as others did. He said Stewart was too blasted uppity; he was an irrascible old cuss. He did sell to the Masons and went east to live with his son. The Masons gel along with Stewart, just as they get along with everybody, including the Harguses. Cart visits at the Slash S ranchhouse quite a bit. I've a notion he sort of likes Stewart's daughter, Ellen, and that she sort of likes him. He's a good-looking young feller and well spoke. The Masons are good cowmen; fixed that rundown old spread up real nice. They 'tend to their own business and don't bother nobody. Wes plays a good game of poker and spends lots of his spare time in the Four Deuces at a table. Neither one of them drink much. Wes and Tom Hargus were friendly and Wes never believed Tom was guilty. Used to go see him regular when Tom was locked up. The Masons are the quiet sort. Guess that's why they get along with Stewart, and why the Harguses don't; *they're* a long ways from being quiet. The Masons respect Stewart, and the Harguses never did.'

The sheriff paused, and there was a twinkle in his eyes. 'Son,' he said, 'I've a notion I haven't talked this much to anybody in a year, but you're a darn good listener and there's something about you that sort of makes a feller want to loosen the latigo on his jaw.'

A quality of Walt Slade's that others before the sheriff had noted.

'And you're a good talker,' Slade said, with a smile. 'I've enjoyed your narration and found it very interesting.'

'Glad you think so,' chuckled Barnes. 'I was beginning to figure I'd bent your ears plumb out of shape. Well, I'm going to round up my deputy—figure he's drunk at the Golconda down the street—and pack Tom's carcass to Doc Cooper's office so he can perform an autopsy on him. You going over to join the Harguses and the Masons?'

38

'I think I'll drop over and have a drink with them and something to eat,' Slade said. 'First, though, I want to find a place to put up my horse.'

'Good livery stable around the next corner and down the alley,' replied the sheriff. 'Tell Grumley, who runs it, I sent you. I may see you at the Four Deuces later.'

Slade located the livery stable without difficulty. Suitable accommodations were provided for Shadow and he himself obtained a small sleeping room over the stalls, where he deposited his saddle and other gear.

'Nothing fancy, but clean and no bugs, which is more than you can say for the fleabags they call hotels,' said the keeper. 'I sleep right next door to you if you should happen to want anything. Sort of chary about renting out this extra room, but if Barnes sent you, you must be okay. Here's a key to the front door; it's always locked at night. Be seeing you; I'm going to bed.'

Slade paused to commune with Shadow a moment before leaving the stable.

'Horse, I sure got a break,' he told the big black. 'I'd been beating my brains out to figure a way to contact Blaine Stewart. And it works out so I get it handed to me on a silver platter, as it were. Things couldn't have worked out better. Yes, I sure got a break.'

Shadow snorted.

Slade smiled, and left.

Four

The Four Deuces proved to be a large and well-outfitted saloon and restaurant combined. There was a dance floor, a long lunch counter and a longer bar. Tables were provided for leisurely eaters, and plenty of gaming tables for poker and other pasteboard diversions. Two roulette wheels, a faro bank, and a chuck-a-luck table offered variety for those who wished to get rid of their money in a hurry.

The Mason brothers were sitting at a table with sandwiches before them when Slade entered. Andy Hargus stood at the bar glooming over his glass. His expression brightened when he spotted Slade and he waved a cordial greeting.

'Come on and have a drink, Slade,' he invited. 'That's your handle, isn't it? Reckon you know mine.' He extended a huge paw and they shook hands.

'Reckon it's up to me to thank you for what you did, even though you came darn near busting my back,' Hargus said. 'I know I shouldn't have lined sights with Stewart that way, but when that old hellion came in I saw red. Guess I get mad too easy and don't use my brains, if I've got any.'

'Do you really believe Blaine Stewart is responsible for your brother's killing?' Slade

40

asked. Hargus was silent a moment, then his answer was rather surprising.

'To tell the truth, after thinking it over, I'm not sure,' he admitted. 'Much as I dislike the old rapscallion, I somehow can't see him going in for cold-blooded murder. But I don't feel that way about that blasted Joe Callison; I figure him capable of anything.'

'Hargus,' Slade asked, 'would your brother have permitted Callison to get close enough to him to shove a gun against his ribs?'

'Heck, no!' exclaimed Hargus. 'He'd have thrown down on the hellion when he was forty feet away.'

'Then Callison didn't kill your brother,' Slade said.

Andy Hargus stared at him. 'Why in blazes do you say that?'

'Because,' Slade said quietly, 'Tom Hargus was killed by someone who was close enough to him to burn his shirt with the gun that killed him. The powder burns on his shirt are plain to see; the sheriff agreed with me that the gun muzzle was smack against Tom's ribs when the killer pulled trigger.'

Hargus looked dazed. 'You—you're sure—about that?' he stuttered.

'Yes, I'm sure, and as I just told you, so is the sheriff,' Slade replied. 'Incidentally, what kind of a gun does Callison pack? I think I know, but I'd like your corroboration.'

'Colt .45, single-action,' Hargus instantly

replied. 'One of those nine-inch barrel hoglegs,' he added. 'You don't see many of 'em.'

'That's right,' Slade said, 'and if Tom had been shot by a Forty-five with a nine-inch barrel, the slug would have gone through him. As it is, the bullet is still in his body. That the only kind of gun you've known Callison to pack?'

'Guess that's right,' replied Hargus. 'Fact is, I'd be willing to swear to it.'

'Then,' said Slade, 'it looks like we can eliminate Cason as a suspect.'

'Then who in blazes did shoot Tom?'

Slade shrugged his broad shoulders. 'You're acquainted with the section, and I'm not,' he pointed out. 'It would seem you are better able to answer that question.'

'Well, I can't,' growled Hargus. 'Of course it could have been one of Stewart's bunch he sicked on Tom. Nope, that won't hold water, either. I'd be willing to swear, too, that Callison wouldn't have somebody else do his revenging for him; he just isn't that sort. He'd get his kind of satisfaction from plugging a feller through the guts and sitting down and watching him die sweatin'. That would be Callison all over.'

'So we're right back where we started,' Slade smiled.

'Uh-huh, only I'm a bit gladder you kept me from plugging Stewart,' Hargus declared.

42

'And I'm glad to hear you say it,' Slade said. 'In fact, my advice to you is to forget all about Stewart. Holding a grudge never does a man any good. It embitters him, poisons his nature, and can often change a decent person into something quite different.'

'You may have something there,' Hargus conceded soberly. His eyes twinkled.

'You're a funny feller, Slade,' he said. 'I don't know just how to take you. You nearly bust a feller's neck and then, by just talking to him soft and easy, you bring him around to your way of thinking. Nope, I don't know what to make of you, but I'm darned glad I met you.'

'Thank you,' Slade said. 'I consider that a compliment. I hope you'll never have cause to regret it.'

'I won't,' Hargus said with decision. 'And I've a notion you might even be able to talk old Blaine Stewart into being something decent 'stead of the ornery old shorthorn he is. Why don't you try it?'

'I may, if I get a chance,' Slade replied laughingly.

'I've a notion you'll get the chance,' said Hargus. 'I'll say this for the old horned toad, he never forgets when somebody does him a good turn, and I reckon right about now he's figuring you did him a real good one, otherwise he'd be explaining to the Devil that he doesn't like the sort of spread he runs.'

Slade laughed again; he found Andy Hargus' manner of expressing himself quite amusing. He had been watching the door and at that moment noticed a man who entered, a very distinguished looking man; tall, slender, straight as an arrow, with graying hair, alert, dark eyes in a bronzed face and a well-shaped but tight mouth. He heard Hargus grunt at his elbow.

'There comes another one of Stewart's bunch,' the Bradded H owner remarked. 'Not such a bad sort, though; everybody likes him. That's Hodson Vane, the editor and publisher of Stewart's newspaper. The *Herald*. He's got connections with other newspaper publishers, too. A smart man, all right.'

Slade eyed Hodson Vane with interest. The editor crossed the room to where the Mason brothers were sitting and drew up a chair.

'The Masons get along with Vane, sort of chummy with him,' Hargus remarked. 'Fine fellers, the Masons, they get along with everybody. They're always giving me good advice, too, but somehow they don't do it like you did. Get me sort of riled at times by pointing out that Stewart is too big for me to buck, and that by not trying to get along with him I just make trouble for myself. I don't like to be shoved around by anybody, no matter how big he thinks he is.'

The giant's eyes were getting hot again and Slade adroitly changed the subject.

44

'Vane from around here?' he asked. Hargus shook his head.

'Came here from Dallas, I understand,' he replied. 'Showed up here a little over a year back and stayed at Stewart's place. Everybody thought he was just visiting Stewart. Reckon he wasn't, though. He browsed around for a while, asking questions and learning all about the section. Then all of a sudden Stewart started putting up the *Herald* Building and let folks know he aimed to publish a newspaper and Vane would be the editor. Guess they'd had it figured for quite a while.'

'I see,' Slade said thoughtfully. 'Vane came here about a year back, you said?'

'That's right,' replied Hargus. 'Just a little over a year back. I rec'lect the time, for it was just a little while before the Masons bought their spread from old Harry Arnold. Old Harry, who was quite a character, said one of the reasons he was moving was that darn newspaper. Said the section was getting too dad-blamed civilized for him, that he was going to where a man could stretch his legs. He was a salty oldtimer, all right, one of the old Indian and Mexican fighters.'

The Masons and Hodson Vane were conversing together. Slade saw the editor turn and glance in his direction. A moment later Cart Mason beckoned to him.

'Guess Cart has something to say to you,' remarked Hargus.

Slade nodded and strolled over to the table. Cart Mason stood up.

'Slade,' he said, 'I want you to know Mr. Hodson Vane, the editor of the *Herald*. We were telling him how you saved Stewart's bacon for him.'

Hodson Vane also stood up, and extended a sinewy hand. 'Very glad to know you, Mr. Slade,' he said. 'Mr. Stewart, in addition to being my employer, is one of my most valued friends. I'd have felt very bad had something happened to him. I wish to thank you for what you did in his behalf.'

They shook hands. Vane's grip was firm, his tapering fingers steely. His smile was pleasant, his manner cordial without being effusive. An able and adroit man, Slade catalogued him.

'Got a place to sleep tonight?' Cart Mason asked. 'If you haven't, it isn't far to our ranchhouse, and we'd be glad to have you ride home with us. We're just getting ready to leave.'

'Thanks,' Slade replied, 'but I've got a room over the stalls at Grumley's livery stable. Sheriff Barnes recommended him.'

'Grumley is all right, a cantankerous cuss but a square-shooter,' Mason nodded. 'I've slept there—good bed.' He sat down again. Vane also resumed his chair. Slade returned to Andy Hargus at the bar.

From time to time men came over to shake hands with Hargus and express regret at his

46

brother's death. To each Slade was introduced.

'Small owners from over the east half of the valley,' Hargus explained. 'Stewart claimed all that land, but it was open range and he neglected to get title. All of a sudden a big speculating outfit over east bought it from the state and parceled it out to small cowmen who wanted to move to this section. Stewart didn't like it a little bit, but he'd waited a mite too long and there was nothing he could do about it. Those fellers don't cotton much to him and his notions of saying how the whole section should be run. The feller who just left, Clyde Hartsook, is a sort of leader of the little fellows.' He gestured to a lean, sinewy, middle-aged man with cold, dead eyes and a thin gash of mouth stretching across his swarthy face. 'I happen to know something about him most folks here don't know. He used to belong to the Brocius gang over in Arizona, before Curly Bill got killed or trailed his twine to Mexico, nobody seems to know for sure which, and the gang busted up. Hartsook got married and reformed and settled down to honest ranching; but he's still a cold, cold proposition. I wouldn't want to have him on my trail. If Stewart aggravates him too much, all his money and the fifty and better hands he has riding for him are liable not to do him any good.'

Slade nodded soberly. Another nice complication added to a situation already too

47

complicated: a range war in the making.

Hodson Vane and the Masons got up and left the saloon, waving good night to Slade and Hargus. Andy ordered another drink and chuckled.

'I'd figured to get blind roaring drunk tonight, but after talking with you I decided not to. I'm going to make this a nightcap and go to bed. I've sent one of my boys who happened to be in town to tell my brother Hank what happened to Tom. He'll be with me at the inquest tomorrow and you'll meet him.'

'Okay,' Slade said. 'I think you're showing good judgment. I'm ready to go when you are. I aim to pound my ear a while, too; didn't get much sleep last night.'

They parted on the street, Hargus heading for the Cattleman's Hotel, where he had a room, Slade proceeding in the other direction to Grumley's livery stable. He reached the alley, dimly lighted now by a vagrant beam from a street lamp, and turned the corner. A few steps from the stable door, he sensed movement in the shadows ahead. Instinctively he slewed sideways. A gun blazed and Slade pitched forward on his face. Through the mists swathing his brain he heard a patter of footsteps, then two shots in quick succession; no lead came close to him. He did not fully lose consciousness, but the slug that grazed his head paralyzed his limbs for the moment. He

48

couldn't move hand or foot.

Dimly, he realized that somebody was kneeling beside him. Hands levered under his shoulders. The man grunted with strain as he heaved the ranger over on his back, muttering to himself. Slade caught the words.

'Just creased! Poor shooting!'

Through slitted lids Slade gazed upward. The man bending over him was Joe Callison, the Slash S range boss.

Five

Callison was still muttering, his voice anxious. 'Come out of it, feller,' he urged. 'You ain't bad hurt; try to sit up.'

With more grunts, Callison managed to raise Slade to a sitting position. The numbness was leaving his arms and legs. He breathed deeply, opened his eyes.

'That's better,' said Callison. 'How you feel?'

'Better,' Slade replied, convinced that Callison meant him no harm.

'I was scairt you were a goner when I saw you go down,' Callison said. 'I was heading for the stable, too, to get my cayuse; always leave him with Grumley. I saw the gun flash and saw you tumble over. I cut loose at the hellion as he hightailed, but I reckon he kept on going.

I'll see in a minute. Think you can stand up?'

Slade answered by lurching to his feet, to stand weaving. His brain was clearing but his head ached and there was a ringing in his ears.

'What the devil's going on down there?' a voice suddenly demanded from somewhere in the air. A double click of gun hammers emphasized the question.

Glancing up, Slade saw the stablekeeper leaning out of an upstairs window, a cocked double-barreled shotgun in his hands.

'It's me, Callison,' the range boss called back.

'What do you mean by kicking up a ruckus at this time of night?' demanded Grumley with a profane qualification as to the region. 'Who's that with you?'

'It's Slade, the feller who left his horse here,' answered Callison. 'Somebody took a shot at him.'

'Somebody's always taking a shot at somebody in this blasted section,' grumbled Grumley. 'You fellers coming in?'

'No,' Callison replied. 'Not yet. I want Slade to go see Doc Cooper. You can't tell about a head injury. Doesn't look to be much, but it could be. Come on, Slade, you'd better have it looked at. Could be a fracture, you know.'

'All right,' Slade agreed. He was not much concerned about the trifling injury, but it was a good chance to contact Doc Cooper, which he wished to do for reasons of his own.

50

'All right,' he repeated, 'and it's nice of you to look after me this way, Callison.'

'And it was nice of you to save the Old Man from getting his comeuppance,' said Callison. 'If it hadn't been for your quick thinking, and handling that blasted Hargus like you did, he'd be stretched out stiff in Doc's office about now. I'm not forgetting it. Come along, let me take your arm.

'We'll be back later, Grumley,' he called to the stablekeeper.

'And try and come in without kicking up another blankety-blank-blank row,' Grumley requested as he banged the window shut.

The walk to the doctor's office was short. Although it was now quite late, a light burned behind closed shutters. Callison hammered on the door.

'Dad blast it! don't knock it down!' bawled an irascible voice. 'Push it open and come in!'

Callison did so to reveal a bristle-whiskered, bristle-haired old fellow with searching eyes under white tufts of brows. The eyes narrowed the merest trifle as they rested on Slade, but the expression of the wrinkled face did not change.

'Well, now what?' the doctor demanded. 'You get your hide punctured again?'

'Not me this time, Doc,' the range boss replied. 'This is Slade, the feller who saved the Old Man from getting killed by that infernal Andy Hargus—guess you heard about it.

Somebody took a shot at him in the alley by Grumley's livery stable; creased him. I figured you ought to take a look at it.'

'You figured right,' grunted Cooper. 'Can't tell about a head injury. Sit down here, Slade, and let me give you a once-over.'

The gnarled old fingers probed the slight cut gently, then stepped back and reached for a bandage and some adhesive tape.

'Doesn't appear to be serious,' he announced. 'But I'll patch him up, give him a sedative and keep him here for a while just to make sure. Much obliged for bringing him in, Callison.'

'And thank you again,' Slade said as the range boss turned to the door.

Callison waved a deprecating hand. 'See you tomorrow at the inquest,' he said. 'The Old Man will be in, too; I figure he'd like to have a talk with you, Slade. Good night.'

After Callison departed, Doc Cooper walked to the door and locked it. Then he turned to Slade with a grin and held out his hand.

'How are you, Walt?' he said. 'Glad to see you. Guess any doctor would be. Business sure picks up in a hurry when you hit town. What the devil are you here for?'

'I've a notion you can guess,' Slade answered as they shook hands.

'Yes, I expect I can,' Cooper nodded.

'But what are you doing here?' Slade asked.

'I thought I left you in Laredo.'

'Oh, folks were getting too dad-blamed healthy over there,' the doctor explained. 'I was being arrested regularly each month for vagrancy—no visible means of support. So I came over here where there's plenty of business. Will be plenty more now, I figure, with you in the section. The undertaker will be the jigger who'll get rich, though.'

'Wouldn't be surprised, if the last few hours are a sample,' Slade agreed, accepting the explanation that did not explain.

Old as he was, Doc Cooper still had itchy feet and could never stay long in one place. He had an outstanding reputation as a practitioner that extended all over Texas and into neighboring states, but he always had to be on the go. This Slade knew and was little surprised to run into him most anywhere. They were old friends and Cooper had more than once rendered valuable assistance when some problem was plaguing the ranger. Slade was very glad to find him located in Alforki Valley.

'Dave Barnes told me you kept Andy Hargus from plugging Blaine Stewart,' Doc remarked. 'I don't figure you did the community or the state a favor. You should have let 'em do for each other for the good of all and sundry.'

'Perhaps I should have,' Slade conceded. 'That's one of the drawbacks in being a law enforcement officer; you have to try to prevent a crime from being committed.'

'Ain't so sure it would have been a crime,' grunted Cooper. 'So you're here to put the kibosh on Stewart's little scheme to do away with the rangers, eh? I reckon you'll do it, but don't underestimate him. He's shrewd and resourceful with plenty of dinero, and he packs influence over to the capital. And the *Herald* isn't the only paper he controls; he's got an interest in a string of them across the state. He's been piling up money and making contacts for years with this thing in mind, and figures that now he can put it over. And that feller Hodson Vane who puts out the *Herald* for him is smart, mighty smart.'

'Wonder where Stewart tied onto him?' Slade remarked.

'Over at Dallas, I understand,' Cooper replied. 'He was working for a paper over there and owned a little cow ranch. Stewart met him somehow, decided he was the man he wanted and persuaded him to come here and put out the Herald. I don't think Vane takes much interest in Stewart's row with the rangers, but he works for Stewart and of course does what Stewart wants him to do. Seems to be a pretty decent sort, so far as I've been able to judge. I've a notion Stewart pays him plenty.'

Slade nodded, and changed the subject. 'You have Tom Hargus here, haven't you?' he asked.

'Yes, he's laid out in the back room,' Cooper replied.

'Good!' Slade said. 'I want you to get the slug out of him; I'd like to have a look at it.'

'You're always having a look at things, and making work for me in one way or another, though when you throw down on some hellion it's usually a job for the undertaker instead of a doctor,' Cooper grumbled.

Nevertheless, he led the way to the back room and went to work on the body, from which he soon recovered the battered bit of lead.

'Was lying alongside the backbone,' he said. 'Nicked a couple of big veins. Hargus slowly bled to death. Quite a bit of time must have elapsed before he got weak enough to tumble over.'

'So I figured,' Slade said, turning the bullet over between his slim fingers. 'This is just as I thought, Doc. Get your scales and let's weigh it.'

A moment later he nodded with satisfaction as the doctor announced the weight in grains registered by the delicate scales.

'That's it, a Forty-one,' he said. 'Yes, a Forty-one.'

'And what does that mean?' asked Cooper.

'It's liable to mean plenty—to somebody,' Slade re-turned grimly. 'You don't see that calibre often in this section, and when you do it's most generally a special kind of iron. Packs a wallop but hasn't the penetrating power of a Forty-five with a long barrel. If Hargus had been shot with a Forty-five at close range, the slug would have gone through instead of stopping on the way.'

'That's right,' the doctor agreed.

Slade stood deep in thought for some minutes, turning the bullet over and over in his hand. Abruptly he asked a question, 'Doc, what do you know about Joe Callison, Stewart's range boss?'

'Good cowman but salty and vindictive,' Cooper replied. 'Poisonous sort of sidewinder, all right, when he's got it in for somebody. I took care of him last year when Tom Hargus drilled him through the shoulder. He swore he'd kill Hargus if he ever got the chance, and he meant it. It was touch and go for a while whether I'd be able to save his arm. Reckon that arm hasn't been over-much good ever since. The slug turned and glanced off the head of the humerus and splintered it. Nasty job.'

'Which would make it appear that Callison figured he had reason for killing Hargus,' Slade observed.

'I reckon so,' Cooper agreed. 'He did come nigh to killing him that day; creased him deep. I reckon he figured Hargus was done for and was too knocked out himself to make sure before he rode to the ranchhouse for help. When Stewart and the sheriff got to where

56

Callison told them the body was lying, they found Tom Hargus still alive. Do you think Callison killed him yesterday?'

Slade shook his head. 'No, I'm pretty sure Callison didn't,' he replied. 'In my opinion, Tom Hargus was killed by somebody he knew and trusted. Somebody who was able to get close enough to him to shove the gun against his ribs. Hargus had no notion he was going to be shot. If you'll look close, you'll see there is an expression of surprise and horror frozen on his dead face.'

Cooper gazed at the rigid countenance of the corpse. 'Darned if I don't believe you're right,' he muttered. 'I don't think I would have noticed it, but now that you point it out, I do. Have you any notion who killed him?'

'If I have, I sure couldn't prove it,' Slade replied evasively. 'Looks like, along with everything else, I've got a murder mystery on my hands.'

'Then you must be plumb happy,' grunted Cooper. 'You're always chipper as a chipmunk when things are at their worst. What are you going to do next?'

'I think I'll try and tie onto a job of riding with Stewart, and I think I can, after what happened last night,' Slade replied.

'Going to settle down in the sidewinder nest, eh?" snorted Cooper.

'There I can keep tabs on him, and maybe change his way of thinking,' Slade said. 'Don't forget, an owl lives in a hole along with a sidewinder, and he's credited with being a pretty smart bird.'

'So I've heard tell,' conceded the doctor. 'But about the only thing that'll change Blaine Stewart's way of thinking is a single-tree or a shotgun, in my opinion.'

'Remains to be seen,' Slade returned cheerfully. 'By the way, put a bug in the sheriff's ear and tell him not to spread the calibre of that bullet around.'

'I'll do it,' Cooper promised. 'He'll listen to me. How's your head feel?'

'Okay,' Slade answered. 'I'm going to bed.'

'Any idea why somebody took a shot at you?'

'There's just a chance that the word has gotten around that *El Halcon* is in town and has made somebody jumpy,' Slade replied noncommitally.

'Wouldn't be surprised,' nodded Cooper. 'If so, you'll hear of it before long.'

'Expect you're right,' Slade answered, still cheerful. 'Fact is, I rather hope so.'

'Why?'

'Because jumpy folks sometimes get careless.'

'Still able to shoot pretty well,' Doc remarked dryly.

'Not quite good enough, though,' Slade said. 'And perhaps what happened tonight will keep me from being so darned careless; I

58

should have been on my guard instead of walking into a drygulching like a dumb yearling. See you tomorrow at the inquest; I'm plumb tuckered out.'

'You should be,' said Cooper. 'Good night.'

Six

Too weary even to think, Slade went to bed and slept soundly. Old Grumley, the stablekeeper greeted him with a curious glance the following morning.

'So, came purty nigh to eating lead, eh?' he remarked. 'Some ornery sidewinder with a notion to lift one of the horses, I reckon. That big black of yours is about the finest looking cayuse I ever laid eyes on. Wouldn't be surprised if somebody else laid eyes on him.'

'I wish they'd tried to lay a hand on him,' Slade replied grimly. 'There wouldn't have been enough left of the jigger to hold an inquest over.'

Grumley nodded agreement. 'Noticed when you brought him in that you gave me the okay first off,' he remarked. 'I like that kind of a horse, and I get along with all kinds. Trough in the back if you'd like a good wash. Soap and towels there, too. Help yourself.

'By the way,' he added as Slade started for the rear of the stable, 'you strike me as a right

59

hombre, no matter what some folks may say. Feller who rides that sort of horse and gets a greeting from him like you did when you come in has to be, so I just want to tip you off it might be a good notion to fight shy of the sheriff's office. I've a notion *he's* heard something, too.'

Slad gazed down at the old fellow and the little devils of laughter in the back of his cold eyes danced; but at the moment they were very kindly devils.

'Thank you, Mr. Grumley, I won't forget it,' he said. Grumley grunted, and busied himself with a pitchfork.

After a sluice in the cold water, Slade felt much better, and ravenously hungry. He repaired to the Four Deuces and ate a leisurely breakfast. After which, despite Grumley's friendly warning, he dropped in on Sheriff Barnes, to find that peace officer in anything but a good temper.

'Sol' he rumbled, with a portentious frown. 'As if I didn't have troubles enough, you have to show up here.'

'How's that?' Slade asked innocently.

The sheriff snorted like a bull with his tail caught on a barbed wire fence.

'I suppose I'm to be plumb pert and happy that *El Halcon*, the owlhoot, has picked my bailiwick to coil his twine in,' he remarked sarcastically.

Slade grinned and sat down, uninvited.

'Well, now's the time to haul out your reward notices and cash in,' he observed.

'Oh, shut up!' grunted the sheriff. 'You know darn well there ain't no reward notices out for you. Nobody seems to be able to tie anything on you. But I got hopes—maybe I'll be the first.'

Abruptly his bad-tempered old face split in a grin as youthful as Slade's.

'Don't know for sure what you are,' he said, 'but I've a feeling that where the owlhoot business is concerned you're phony as a seven-dollar bill. I've heard a lot about you and got to taking a mite of interest in your shenanigans. The jiggers I've heard you cashed in read like the State Prison up for roll call. But don't forget, son, there are other folks who don't feel that way and may hanker for a chance to make trouble for you. I'm not so sure Andy Hargus feels overkind to you for keeping him from plugging Blaine Stewart. And there's another Hargus brother who, in my opinion, is the coldest proposition of the three of them. Hank's the quiet one. Andy is a drinker, to an extent, and Tom was a loco gambler. Hank ain't got any bad habits at all, so far as anybody's been able to notice, so I figure he's the one to watch. By the way, Joe Callison told me what happened at the stable last night. See what I mean?'

'Yes, I see,' Slade conceded soberly.

'Callison said he went back after getting you

61

to the doctor and combed that alley and didn't find anything,' the sheriff resumed. 'Said he must have missed the blankety-blank in his flurry; didn't find any blood spots, and there isn't much that half-Indian doesn't see. You got any notion who did it?'

'None,' Slade replied. 'But only a very few people, aside from yourself, knew I intended to sleep in Grumley's stable, and I'm sort of eliminating you, which is as far as I care to go right now.' The sheriff nodded.

'Always best not to go sounding off about something till you're sure,' he commended. 'Anyhow I figure you've got a friend in Callison. He thinks a lot of old Blaine.

'Of course, the jigger who took a shot at you might have been somebody whose toes you tromped in some other section,' the sheriff hazarded.

Slade neither conceded nor denied.

'Inquest will be held in Doc Cooper's office in an hour,' the sheriff added. 'I'll see you there. Right now I've got to go and make ready for it. Stewart will be there, and the Harguses, and a lot more folks. Stick around here in the office till the time, if you're of a mind to.'

With a nod he headed for the street, leaving Slade smoking thoughtfully.

With the Harguses and their hands present, and Blaine Stewart and a number of his also present, Sheriff Barnes took no chances with the inquest. He issued no warnings, voiced no threats; but he swore in ten special deputies. These, armed to the teeth, lounged about the room and kept a watchful eye on proceedings.

The room was crowded and there was an overflow onto the street. Slade noted that the Mason brothers and a number of townspeople clumped together with Stewart and the dozen riders he had brought with him. Another contingent in rangeland clothes grouped together. Evidently representatives of the small ranchers to the east, who were evincing a lively interest in the affair. Already there was a taking of sides; trouble in the making. But for the moment the sheriff and his ten armed specials had the situation well in hand, and there were no demonstrations.

The inquest didn't take long. Slade told of finding the body and the Mason brothers confirmed the details. No mention was made of Slade's initial run-in with the Masons, both he and the brothers tacitly agreeing that nothing would be gained by doing so and there was no sense in injecting any controversial matter into the hearing.

The jury's verdict was short and to the point. Tom Hargus met his death at the hands of a party or parties unknown. The sheriff was advised to run the varmints down and bring them to justice.

Outside the office, Stewart and his bunch turned to the left and walked unhurriedly down the street.

'They're headed for the Golconda Saloon, where they often hang out,' Sheriff Barnes said to Slade. 'The others will go to the Four Deuces. I intend to make it my business to see that they stay apart while they're in town. My boys have their orders and will see to it that they do. There are the Harguses waving to you. Reckon Andy wants to introduce you to his brother. Drop in at the office, when you're finished with them.'

Hank Hargus was about half the size of his brother, and although there was a resemblance, Slade quickly concluded that in disposition they were the antithesis of each other. Hank, unlike the impulsive, quick-tempered Andy, would weigh and assess and study all angles of a proposition before committing himself to a plan of action. He acknowledged the introduction courteously and shook hands in an impersonal way. Slade felt that he was holding his judgment in abeyance.

'Glad you kept Andy from making a fool of himself last night,' he said; 'he's always going off half-cocked. The Mason boys try hard to keep him out of trouble, but they don't have much luck.'

Andy Hargus snorted. 'He's got icewater in his veins instead of blood,' he growled, apropos of his brother. 'Not that it can't heat up when he's of a mind for it to. Come on and

64

let's have a drink.'

'I'll join you a little later,' Slade declined. 'Right now I want to have a talk with the sheriff.'

Andy Hargus shot him a peculiar look, Hank a speculative one, but neither commented.

'Be seeing you, then. We'll be at the Four Deuces,' Andy said. 'Come along, Hank.'

Slade found Sheriff Barnes sitting at his desk, smoking his pipe. He nodded and gestured to one of the repaired chairs. Slade sat down and rolled a cigarette.

'Just who told you I was *El Halcon?*' the ranger asked.

'Barkeep at the Four Deuces mentioned it,' Barnes replied. 'He said it was all over town. Don't know just who it was spotted you.'

Slade nodded and lighted his cigarette. For some time they smoked in silence. The sheriff was about to speak when the door opened and Blaine Stewart entered, with him a wizened and cantankerous individual whom Slade judged to be about a hundred-and-seventy-five years old, although after a moment of reflection he decided to knock off the hundred. However, his beady black eyes were quick and alert, his movements assured.

Stewart waved to the sheriff. 'Howdy, Slade,' he said. 'This is Charley Simpson, my cook. He was with my Dad before he passed on.'

65

'He wasn't a blasted fool like you,' interjected Simpson, shooting a contemptuous glance at his employer and extending a gnarled paw for Slade to shake.

'I've had to put up with that for forty years and better,' sighed Stewart. 'I don't know why I do.'

'Because if you hadn't, you'd have been dead for forty years, or in jail for that long,' snapped Simpson. 'Go ahead and do what I told you to.'

'It's like this,' Stewart said, almost apologetically. 'Charley heard about you and at the inquest he sized you up and 'lowed it would be a good notion—'

'I did not,' the irascible Simpson interjected flatly. 'I told you to sign him up with the Slash S, if you can get him to agree.'

'I guess that's about the size of it,' Stewart admitted sheepishly. 'What do you say, Slade? I pay top wages. First I'd like to ask you something—are you *El Halcon*?'

'Been called that,' Slade admitted.

'And I suppose the blasted rangers take an interest in you, eh?'

'Somewhat,' Slade agreed smilingly.

'That's enough for me,' Stewart declared heartily. 'Say the word and you're on the payroll, as of yesterday.'

'Well, sir,' Slade said, 'I guess you've hired yourself a hand.'

'Fine!' exclaimed Stewart. 'Let's go have a

drink on it.'

'Later,' Slade said. 'I promised the Harguses I'd meet them in the Four Deuces.'

Blaine Stewart's face darkened. 'All right,' he said shortly. 'See you later. Come on, Charley!'

'You get the heck back to the Golconda,' replied that worthy. 'I'm going to the Four Deuces with Slade.'

'Okay,' sighed Stewart.

'Charley used to larrup the blinkin' blue blazes outa him when he was a tad and Blaine ain't never forget it,' the sheriff remarked *sotto voce* as Slade paused a moment before following the others. 'He sets a heap of store by the old feller's judgment. In my opinion, Charley has the most brains of the two; he can even quiet Andy Hargus down if he gets to him in time. He gets along with everybody and don't play no favorites. Good notion for you to sign up with Stewart. Time you were settling down instead of maverickin' around and maybe getting into bad trouble. Be seeing you.'

Slade found old Charley waiting for him outside; Stewart had taken his departure. Andy Hargus and Hank were at the bar when they entered the Four Deuces. 'Howdy, Charley,' Andy called.

'Another dad-burned fool!' snorted Simpson. 'Hank has a few brains.'

Andy grinned and ordered him a drink. Charley swallowed it at a gulp, as if it were so much water, and placed his glass on the bar for a refill.

'See you've taken Slade in tow,' Andy said, motioning to the bartender.

'Yep,' said Simpson. 'Signed him up. Will be nice to have a real hand around after the terrapin-brained misfits we have to put up with. When you going to bury poor Tom? I'll be there. Slade will come, too.'

'Tomorrow afternoon,' Andy replied sadly. 'Let's have another drink.'

Slade noticed Wes Mason sitting at a nearby poker table. He observed with interest Mason's skill in shuffling and dealing. Wes was wooden-faced and appeared cool as a horned toad on ice. Slade concluded that he played a good game of cards and handled the pasteboards like a professional dealer in big games. An entirely different type of player than what he had gathered of Tom Hargus, who evidently had had the gambling fever bad. He glanced around the crowded room but failed to locate Cart Mason.

'Here comes Hodson Vane,' Hargus remarked. 'Reckon he'll sit in that game. It's a big one, and he likes to play.'

'Another dang fool, but a smart one,' snorted old Charley, downing a second drink and hammering on the bar.

'Fill 'em up, on me, and have one yourself,' he told the drink juggler.

Slade watched Vane make his way to the

poker table, his step lithe, his bearing graceful, assured. A fine looking man, all right. He wondered if Charley's remark was only the cantankerous maundering of the very old or if it had some hidden meaning understood only by the shrewd cook who certainly did not look or act as if he were approaching second childhood. Well, most everybody had a weakness or a foible of some sort; there might be a facet in Vane's character of which Simpson did not approve. Gambling, perhaps. For as he watched Vane manipulate the cards he concluded that he was no stranger to poker.

Slade, who was ultra-sensitive to such things, had a feeling that eyes were watching him. Without turning his head, he slanted his own eyes sideways. A moment later his oblique glance fixed on Clyde Hartsook, said by Andy Hargus to have once been one of the Curly Bill Brocius outlaws and now the acknowledged leader of the small ranchers to the east. He realized it was Hartsook's concentrated stare that had impressed itself on his acute sensibilities. Hartsook had evidently been studying him intently.

At that moment, however, the rancher's gaze shifted to Hodson Vane at the poker table, and Slade could see that Hartsook's intense concentration had focused on the *Herald* editor. Moreover, his dead-looking eyes narrowed and there was a cynical quirking of his thin, reptilian mouth. A moment later he

69

shrugged his shoulders and turned back to the bar. Slade wondered what the bit of byplay he had witnessed meant. Something had amused Hartsook, amused him in a derisive way. And he didn't look to be a man who was easily amused.

Slade saw the silent Hank Hargus approach Hartsook; they conversed earnestly for several minutes, then Hank joined his brother. He nodded cordially to Slade and old Charley.

'Guess we'd better be going,' he said to Andy. 'We've got things to do.'

'Yes, I reckon we have,' Andy returned heavily. 'Have the boys got the wagon ready?'

'Ready and loaded,' replied Hank. 'Let's go.'

'See you tomorrow at two, then,' Andy said to Slade. 'So long.'

Slade watched the brothers depart on their dreary errand. Old Charley finished his drink.

'Guess we'd better head for the Golconda and see if those varmints have managed to get into trouble while I wasn't there to keep an eye on 'em,' said Charley.

Stewart and his hands were drinking at the Golconda. bar. The Golconda was rather more pretentious than the Four Deuces, and quieter. Evidently the Slash S bunch had kept out of trouble even without old Charley's supervising eye.

'Riding to the spread with us?' Stewart asked of Slade.

'I'm staying in town tonight,' the ranger replied. 'I promised Andy Hargus I'd attend his brother's funeral tomorrow.'

Blaine Stewart frowned. 'I don't exactly approve of the Harguses, as you may be able to guess,' he remarked.

Slade let his level eyes rest on the ranchowner's face, 'Mr. Stewart,' he said, 'when I'm working for a man, I work for him, but he doesn't dictate to me what I do in my off time.'

Stewart flushed, but perhaps something in the cold eyes boring into his gave him pause.

'Okay,' was all he said. Old Charley chuckled.

Seven

They buried young Tom Hargus on the hillside beneath the whispering pines, where there were already many graves, some nameless, some with leaning headstones and the quaint lettering of bygone years. A large crowd attended the funeral, for the small ranchowners from the east of the valley turned out en masse with their families. And many curious glances were directed at the tall, black-haired man with the steady gray eyes who stood beside Andy Hargus at the open grave.

'That's *El Halcon*,' the whispered comment

ran. 'Some folks say he's an outlaw, but he sure looks like a right hombre to me. They say he kept Andy Hargus from killing Blaine Stewart, outwrestled Andy and then made friends with him. Blazes! Isn't he a fine looking feller!'

An old clergyman who had spent his long life ministering to the people of the Border country came down from Marfa to read the service over Tom Hargus. A hush fell as he opened his Book.

'I am the Resurrection and the Light . . .'

And the peaceful earth fell gently on the coffin like soothing summer rain.

When the clergyman closed his Book he turned to the crowd with a wistful smile on his wrinkled face.

'Now if somebody would just lead a hymn—' he suggested.

'Parson,' called a voice, 'the singingest man in Texas is standing right beside you!'

The minister turned to Slade. 'Would you lead?' he asked gently.

Slade stepped forward, gazed down a moment at the low mound, bare and brown till the new grass was grown. Then his great golden baritone-bass came softly forth in the words of a stirring old hymn that a-down the years has brought comfort and surcease from sorrow to many a grieving soul:

'Home again from a distant shore!'

72

The clergyman gestured to the crowd, and voice after voice took up the refrain to the last inspiring line:

'Home! and rest at last!'

'Thank you, sir, you have a wonderful voice,' the minister said to Slade, and shook hands.

Hank Hargus also extended his hand before walking away with the minister, and this time his clasp was hearty and warm.

Andy Hargus drew a deep breath and when he turned to Slade, his eyes were very bright.

'Now I feel a lot better,' he sighed.

'Yes,' Slade said, 'he has found what all of us seek—the peace that passeth all understanding.'

Slade turned at a touch on his arm to face Cart Mason and a tall girl with rich dark hair and beautiful dark eyes who stood beside him.

'Ellen,' Mason said to his companion, 'I want you to know Walt Slade. Slade, this is Miss Ellen Stewart, Blaine Stewart's daughter.'

Ellen Stewart extended a slender little sun-golden hand over which Slade bowed with courtly grace.

'I've been hearing so much about you, Mr. Slade,' she said. 'And the best I've heard is that you are going to ride for my father.'

El Halcon's white smile, which men, and women, found irresistible, lighted his sternly handsome face.

'And all of a sudden I'm very glad I'm going to,' he said.

The girl blushed prettily and her very lively eyes danced. Instantly they were grave, however, as she turned to Andy Hargus and again held out her hand.

'You have my deepest sympathy, Mr. Hargus,' she said. 'I can understand how you feel. I, too, lost a brother, when I was very young, but I still remember.'

Andy Hargus, who had flushed to the roots of his red hair, hesitated, then engulfed the little hand in his huge paw.

'Th-thank you, Miss Stewart,' he stuttered. 'It was good of you to come.'

'I'm glad I did,' she replied, with a swift smile that showed white, even teeth and a dimple at the corner of her red mouth.

'Ellen, I reckon we'd better be going,' Cart Mason suggested.

'Yes, I suppose so,' she agreed. 'Goodbye, Mr. Hargus. I'll see you at the ranch tomorrow, Mr. Slade.'

Andy Hargus, looking dazed, gazed after her. 'Blazes! Isn't she a wonder!' he rumbled. 'I've seen her before, of course, riding in town or out on the range, but this is the first time close up.'

'A very pretty girl, and a charming one,' Slade agreed.

'Cart Mason sure is lucky,' said Andy, a

touch of envy in his voice.

Slade smiled slightly. 'Perhaps,' he said. Andy glanced at him, but refrained from asking questions.

People began to pass, pausing to shake hands, mostly in silence, for which Slade knew the Harguses were thankful. It is from the presence of others that comfort and support are derived in the dark hours of grief, not from talk, which often only serves to irritate. Before a bad storm, animals herd together, but they cease their calling.

Last to put in an appearance was old Charley Simpson. 'Guess we'd better be moseying, Slade,' he said. 'We've got a long ride ahead of us.'

'Come to the house first for a cup of coffee and a snack,' Andy insisted.

'All right,' Charley agreed, 'but it'll be dark before we get home.'

*   *   *

It was dark quite a while before they reached the great Slash S ranchhouse, and even as they were sighting the grove of ancient oaks in which it sat, an interesting conversation was underway in the big living room which boasted a grand piano, among many other things.

'Well,' Ellen Stewart remarked to her father, 'I met your Mr. Slade at the funeral today.'

'I didn't approve of you going to that funeral,' snorted old Blaine, 'but what did you think of him?'

'I think he is the handsomest man I ever laid eyes on and an extraordinary personality, the kind you don't often meet,' his daughter replied.

''Pears he takes everybody in tow,' old Blaine grumbled. 'He nigh to busted Andy Hargus' neck and then proceeded to tie Andy to the tail of his kite. Charley fell for him head over heels within ten seconds of meeting him, which is a mite out of the ordinary for Charley. I've a notion he's got Dave Barnes plumb hypnotized.'

'I've a notion you have sort of fallen for him yourself,' Ellen smiled.

'Well, blast it, he saved my life, didn't he?' Stewart countered defensively.

'For which I owe him a great debt of gratitude,' his daughter said softly.

'The kind of debt there's no paying off,' Stewart conceded.

'He sang a hymn at the funeral,' Ellen went on. 'I never heard such a voice. It was out of this world.'

'The singingest man in the whole southwest, with the fastest gunhand, they call him,' Stewart observed. 'I've a notion they're right on both counts.'

'I can certainly vouch for the singing part,' Ellen declared. 'Why such a man is working as

76

a cowhand is beyond my comprehension.'

'He talks like an educated feller,' Stewart observed.

'I'll wager that if you manage to learn the truth, you'll find out that he's a college man,' Ellen declared with emphasis.

In which Miss Stewart was eminently correct. Shortly before the death of his father after business reverses that entailed the loss of the elder Slade's ranch, Walt Slade had graduated from a famous college of engineering. His plan had been to take a postgraduate course in specialized subjects to round out his education and better prepare him for the profession he had determined to make his life work. This became impossible for the time being, and Slade found himself somewhat at loose ends.

So when Captain Jim McNelty, the famous commander of the Border Battalion of the Texas Rangers, and his father's friend, with whom Slade had worked some during summer vacations, suggested that he come into the rangers for a while and pursue his studies in spare time, Slade thought it a good idea. Long since, he had gotten more from private study than he could have hoped for from the postgrad and was well fitted for an engineering career.

But ranger work had gotten a strong hold on him and he was loath to sever connections with the illustrious body of law enforcement officers. He was young and there was plenty of time to be an engineer; he'd stick with the rangers for a while.

'I've a notion he could give you a lot of help with the book work you detest,' Ellen remarked with apparent irrelevance. 'And if we could keep him sticking around the house, maybe he'd sing for us now and then. You love music; you'd enjoy it.'

'By gosh, that's an idea!' exclaimed her father. 'And both bunkhouses are a mite crowded right now. We'll just bunk him in one of the spare rooms upstairs.'

His pretty daughter bit back a smile, having very nicely put over her point.

'You're right that he's an extraordinary personality,' Stewart remarked reflectively. 'I'll have to admit that he's got something in his makeup that gets under your hide, especially when he looks at you real hard. You don't know what he's thinking, but it makes you sort of squirm inside, and feel sorta scared that maybe he don't approve, and all of a sudden you don't want him to disapprove. I don't understand what he has about him, but it's something.'

'Dad,' Ellen said, 'do you recall "The Cotter's Saturday Night" by Robert Burns? There's a line I've never forgotten—"An honest man's the noblest work of God."'

'That may be it,' her father returned heavily. 'Some folks say he's an outlaw, but that may be it.'

*   *   *

'I see there's a light burning in the living room,' Charley Simpson remarked as he and Slade reached the ranchhouse yard. 'Reckon the Old Man is still up; after we put up our bronks, we'll drop in and see him before heading for the kitchen and something to eat.'

Blaine Stewart was up when they entered the living room, and so was his daughter. She shot Slade a swift smile and nodded.

'So you made it, eh?' said Stewart.

'Yep, we made it,' answered Simpson. 'I'm going out and rustle us a surrounding; only had a sandwich at the Harguses.' He started across the room, but Ellen stopped him with a peremptory gesture.

'You're tired,' she said. 'I'll make you something to eat. Sit down!'

Old Charley grumbled under his mustache but obediently dropped into a chair.

'I'm the only person in the world he'll take orders from and not argue,' she whispered, her eyes dancing, as she passed Slade.

'So they planted young Hargus,' Stewart remarked, by way of making conversation.

"Yep, they planted him,' Charley returned soberly, shaking his white head. 'I don't know why the young shoots should be pulled, and old weeds like you and me left standing, but I reckon there must be a reason, since the Good Lord plans it that way.'

'My brother was about Tom's age when he was murdered,' Stewart observed with apparent irrelevance.

'Are you sure he was murdered, Mr. Stewart?' Slade asked quietly.

Blaine bristled. 'Of. course I'm sure,' he declared belligerently.

'Just as Andy Hargus was sure you were responsible for his brother's murder,' Slade remarked, adding, also with apparent irrelevance, 'I've a notion he's changed his mind about that.'

Old Blaine glared, but once again something in the ranger's steady eyes caused him to glance away, and change the subject. Charley Simpson chuckled.

'We're going to bunk you in the house,' Stewart announced. 'Ellen will show you your room; I'm going to bed. By the way, perhaps you can help me with the book work? That's a chore I despise. I ain't much good at figures and my handwriting looks like where a hen's been scratching in a dust heap.'

'I'll be glad to,' Slade replied.

'Fine!' said Stewart. 'See you in the morning; good night.'

He stumped up the stairs and a moment later a door banged. Old Charley turned to Slade.

'I don't know what the devil to make of

80

you,' he complained. 'I never heard anybody talk to the Old Man like that, and get away with it. How do you do it?'

Slade smiled, and did not answer.

A few moments later a sweet voice called from the back of the house, 'Come and get it or I'll throw it away!'

Charley hopped to his feet. 'Chuck's on,' he said. 'Let's go, I'm starved.' He led the way to the big dining room, where places were set for three.

'I'm hungry, too,' Ellen announced. 'Sit down, Mr. Slade.'

A knife and a fork sufficed for Charley, but Slade found quite an array of silverware at his place. The layout seemed to amuse him, for his lips quirked at the corners and his eyes crinkled. He casually lifted a misplaced spoon and laid it on the other side of his plate. Then he raised his eyes to Ellen and smiled.

She blushed rosily, but offered no comment; neither did Slade.

They had a very pleasant meal together, for Slade and the girl ate with the appetite of youth and perfect health, and old Charley showed that the years had not abated his ability to put away a hefty surrounding.

'I'll help you with the dishes,' Slade offered after they had finished and he had smoked a cigarette. Charley was smoking his pipe. 'I'm a hired hand now, you know.'

'I don't think Dad hired you to perform

such chores,' she answered. Nevertheless she did not decline the offer. Charley grunted good night and ambled off to bed.

'Quite homelike,' Slade said as the last plate was put away.

'You have no home, Mr. Slade?' she asked.

'I wouldn't say that, so long as I have my saddle for a pillow, the sky for a blanket and the stars and my horse for company,' he differed smilingly.

'That sounds very romantic, but I'm not so sure as to the comfort,' she said. 'Don't you ever get lonely?'

'Learn to live with yourself and you're never lonely,' he replied.

'Yes, I think that is true,' she said as they walked to the living room. 'I think Dad is quite lonely at times. Nearly all his old friends are dead or moved away, and he doesn't get along with the new people who have come to the valley. Sometimes I liken him to Ishmael.'

' "His hand against every man, and every man's hand against him," ' Slade quoted.

'Yes,' she said, a touch of bitterness in her voice, 'and that's not the way to be happy. But I believe you will be a good influence on him; he seems to have taken a great liking to you.'

'I hope it will continue,' Slade said.

'I'm sure it will,' she replied. 'I think that when one likes you, one will always—like you. Though perhaps in some instances with— regret.'

'Now what do you mean by that?' he asked.

She laughed, and did not elaborate on her cryptic remark. 'It's late, and you must be tired after a hard day,' she said. 'I'll show you to your room.'

Near the head of the stairs she opened a door and lit a lamp. 'I hope you'll be comfortable, even without the stars, the sky, and your horse,' she smiled.

'They still exist,' he replied. 'And I'm sure I'll be comfortable,' he added, glancing around the nicely furnished room.

With a nod she crossed the hall to another door and opened it. 'Good night,' she said, and closed the door, very softly.

Eight

Slade was comfortable, so much so that when he awakened with a start, the sun was already pretty well up in the sky. He washed and dressed hurriedly and descended to the living room, where he found Ellen awaiting him.

'Nice way to start on a new job, pounding my ear till nine o'clock,' he said.

'I wouldn't allow you to be disturbed,' she replied. 'You needed your rest. Charley has your breakfast ready, and I waited to eat with you. Dad is out around the barn; he'll be in shortly.'

Stewart put in an appearance soon after they finished eating. After a few minutes' conversation he led Slade to a room which served as an office.

'There you are,' he said, gesturing to a cluttered desk and filing cabinets. 'You can turn your wolf loose on it. I'll see you later; got a few chores outside to do. Ellen will call me if you want anything.'

Very quickly Slade discovered that Stewart's books were in a good deal of a mess. The accounts dealt not only with the big ranch but also with his mining properties and other holdings. Before he got things straightened out fairly well, he was willing to agree that Blaine Stewart was not good at figures. He wondered how much the Old Man was being robbed if he happened to have some unscrupulous underlings in his employ. He was surprised when Ellen came in to tell him to come and eat.

'Where'd the time go?' he wondered.

'I think it's easy to see where it went,' she said, glancing at the neat piles of papers and the figures and notations legible as print. 'Dad will be eternally grateful to you. I try to help him, but like him, I'm not good at figures. I'm afraid I'm more of a hindrance than a help.'

'Impossible!' he replied. 'Your very presence would be an inspiration.'

'Then I'll sit with you tomorrow,' she said with a gay laugh. 'And I'll promise not to talk.

84

Come along or Charley will be bellowing his head off; he doesn't like for things to get cold. Dad's already at the table.'

After the noonday meal was over, Stewart turned to Slade. 'Figure you've been cooped up enough for one day,' he said. 'I aim to ride to town this afternoon; want to see Hodson Vane, the editor of my paper. You come along.'

Slade was not sorry for an opportunity to get out of the stuffy office, so after a smoke he got the rig on Shadow and helped Blaine saddle a big and spirited roan. Ellen was awaiting them at the foot of the veranda when they rode from the barn.

'Oh, what a beautiful horse!' she exclaimed. 'I wonder would he let me ride him?'

'He will if I tell him to,' Slade replied. 'Otherwise he'd very likely stand you on your head in that rose bush, that is if you managed to mount him, which is highly improbable.'

'I'm not so sure of that,' she answered spiritedly. 'I can ride.'

'Don't put it to a test,' he advised. 'Although he is usually very gentle where women are concerned.'

'And I expect he's had plenty of opportunities to be gentle,' she said.

Slade grinned. Blaine chuckled.

'Let's get going,' he said. 'See you later, chick.'

The ride to Alforki was a rather long one,

but Slade enjoyed it. Old Blaine appeared occupied with his own thoughts and spoke but seldom. Mostly in silence they rode, in quiet appreciation of the Autumn beauty of the range. Already there were blotches of vivid color staining the green of the growth. The grasses were purpling, though flowers still bloomed in the moister hollows. Far to the south, high, multi-colored and hazy, the Chisos Mountains bulked in a serrated mass against the horizon. Red, blue, purple and yellow, their hues were like a shattered rainbow fallen to earth and frozen into stone. Barely seen to the southeast were the Carmen Mountains of Mexico, a deep, velvet red, or purplish maroon, the mighty range with heights of eight thousand to ten thousand feet sweeping away for forty miles and more.

The Santiagos towered to the east in rugged grandeur, a continuation of the Rocky Mountain system, with the Cienagas almost due west.

A wild and beautiful land, Slade thought, where most anything could happen, and usually did.

Reaching Alforki, they stabled the horses and then made their way to the *Herald* Building, a hive of activity, vibrating to the thunder of the presses, where the distinguished looking Hodson Vane presided.

When Slade shook hands he sensed the steel of the man. Hodson Vane was a personality, all right, a man to be reckoned with. He was courteous, almost deferential to Blaine Stewart, but Slade quickly concluded that pertaining to matters concerning the *Herald*, Vane led and Stewart followed.

He also concluded, however, that were the old fighter really in earnest about something he could sweep Vane's or anybody else's plans into the wastepaper basket and set his own course, come hell or high water. Vane was a shrewd and calculating diplomat who explored all angles before acting; Stewart a rugged individualist accustomed to hewing his way through opposition with pole-axe blows.

Acting in concert, they were a formidable combination. Slade felt more than ever that the warning he voiced to Captain McNelty not to underestimate the seriousness of the campaign being waged against the rangers was not misplaced.

'Here are some galley proofs I thought you might like to see, Mr. Stewart,' Vane said, passing the long sheets to the rancher.

Blaine took them and slowly spelled out the wording, chuckling as he did so.

'Fine!' he applauded, handing the proofs back to the editor. 'This one'll raise a blister. We've got those hellions on the run and we'll keep 'em that way. The next legislature will get rid of the murdering misfits, see if it don't. Yes, you're doing fine, Vane. I sure tied onto a winner when I picked you.'

Hodson Vane's thin lips twisted in what was apparently intended for a smile, although it never seemed to reach his keen eyes. Slade, smoking a cigarette, seemingly taking no interest in the conversation and gazing out the window, could feel Vane's intensely calculating gaze studying him. Somehow, despite his urbane bearing, the editor appeared to suffer from a certain perturbation, as if here was somebody with whom he might have to seriously reckon. Slade thought that perhaps he resented his familiarity with Blaine Stewart, who showed plainly that he did not look upon him, Slade, as a mere hired hand but more in the nature of a confidant.

Which, after all, was not too surprising. Vane undoubtedly had a good job with Stewart and exerted a certain influence over him. For all he knew Slade might be usurping that influence, to an extent, at least. Vane, not unnaturally, could hardly be expected to take kindly to that.

'Here's a copy of this week's edition,' the editor said. Stewart took the paper, folded it, and shoved it into his coat pocket.

'Read it tonight after I get home,' he said. 'Better light there, and my eyes ain't what they used to be when it comes to close work. I know it's okay, anyhow. As I said, you're doing fine. Keep up the good work. Come on, Slade, let's go get a drink.'

Hodson Vane's eyes followed them as they

left the building, a slight pucker between his brows. He sauntered to his office door and beckoned a man who was idling about a composing stone, a lean-faced, alert-looking individual whose complexion indicated more time spent outdoors than in.

The man nodded and followed Vane into the office, the door of which the editor closed behind him.

Slade and Stewart found the Four Deuces already pretty well crowded. Blaine glanced about with interest. 'There's young Cart Mason over there, playing cards,' he remarked. 'He don't play much. Don't drink much, either. Nice looking feller. He drops around to my place quite often. I've a notion he sort of likes my gal Ellen. A notion maybe she sort of likes him, too. Well, he's just getting a start, but he's a quiet, steady-going young feller and better'n most, I'd say. A heck of a lot different from that blasted fire-eatin' Andy Hargus, for example. Don't you think so?'

Slade turned to face him. 'Are you asking my opinion regarding your daughter and her associates?' he asked.

Old Blaine's eyes widened a little. 'Why—why, I guess that's right,' he said, looking somewhat bewildered.

'Then,' said Slade, 'it's my opinion that Andy Hargus would make her a very good husband and would follow her around and do just what she told him to like a pet lamb.'

Old Blaine stared, his face flushing darkly. For a moment he looked as if he might have a stroke, for he breathed with apparent difficulty.

'Slade,' he demanded, 'are you plumb loco?'

'Nope,' Slade replied.

Old Blaine hammered on the bar, bringing a drink juggler running. He waved him away imperiously.

'If that young whippersnapper ever comes hanging around my place, I'll fill him full of buckshot!' he rumbled.

'I doubt it,' Slade replied composedly. 'Especially if your daughter happens to bring him around.'

'What!' bawled the scandalized rancher in a voice that caused heads to turn inquiringly in his direction. 'Do you mean to say I ain't the boss of my own household?'

'You can't even boss your cook, let alone your daughter, who has a mind of her own and who can, I'm convinced, wrap you around her finger whenever she's of a mind to,' Slade answered smilingly.

Old Blaine gave a hollow groan. 'Slade,' he said, 'arguing with you is like playing tag with a nest of hornets—you can't win!'

'Well, am I not right?' Slade asked, still smiling.

'You could be, I reckon,' old Blaine said heavily. 'Yes, maybe you could be. Oh, heck! Let's have another drink.'

Nine

They had several. Then Stewart decided he'd like to sit in a poker game where some townspeople he knew were playing for small stakes. Slade was invited to sit in too and managed to stay about even. All in all, it was quite late when they left Alforki and headed back to the Slash S ranchhouse.

'Ain't had so much fun for a long time,' Blaine declared as they jogged along under the stars. 'You're good company, Slade.'

'You're not bad yourself, sir, when you haven't got your bristles up,' the ranger replied. Old Blaine chuckled.

'Oh, I have to snort now and then or I'd blow up,' he said. 'Maybe I ain't so bad as I sound.'

'You're not, if you'd only come to realize it,' Slade returned. Stewart looked puzzled. He studied the stars, glanced at the wall of brush on either side which towered above their heads, for here the trail ran through a deep galley for nearly a mile, with dense chaparral fringing the lips of its sides and sometimes almost intertwining over the narrow gulch.

'This darn ditch gets so full of water during a bad rain you can drown yourself,' he remarked. 'The only way then is to circle the brush and keep on the prairie, and that means

91

a few miles out of your way. It's okay most of the time, though, and a good shortcut.'

The night was moonless, but star-bright and very still. The western hills reared their craggy bulk against the spangled sky. The prairie had a ghostly look. Groves and clumps of thicket were black, as if carved from jet, for now they were out of the gulley and could see for some little distance across the range. No wind stirred the grass heads and the popping of saddle leather and jingle of bridle irons sounded strangely loud in the great hush.

Suddenly Slade lifted his head in an attitude of listening.

'Horses coming this way, coming fast,' he said. A moment later, 'No, it isn't horses, it's cows, a lot of them, a hundred or more, I'd say.'

'What the devil would cows be running this time of night for?' sputtered Stewart. 'We're on my land now. Has some of my boys gone loco?'

Slade pulled Shadow to a halt. 'Back your horse into the brush and be ready to grab his nose if he starts to neigh,' he told his companion. 'I don't know what it's all about, but it doesn't look good to me. I want to get a look at things without being seen. Quick, they're getting close.'

Muttering and rumbling, Stewart obeyed. 'Quiet!' Slade told him. 'Sounds carry a long way on a night like this. Quiet, and keep your

92

eyes skinned.'

Tense and alert they waited. The rumble of hoofs loudened. Another moment and the dark mass of the moving cattle hove into view. They swept past, bleating protests. After them surged a tight group of riders.

Just in time Slade caught the gleam of the gun Stewart had drawn. His iron grip closed on the rancher's wrist and he wrenched the weapon from his numbed hand.

'What are you trying to do, commit suicide?' he whispered angrily. 'There are a dozen men in that bunch; we wouldn't have a chance.'

'But those are my cows—couldn't be anybody else's!' Stewart hissed in fury. 'The hellions are runnin 'em off.'

'You won't get them back by being a darn fool,' Slade snapped, for now the herd was past and the pound of hoofs would drown his voice. 'Wait, let me think a moment. I believe I've got it. Back there where the trail runs through that gulch. If we can get there ahead of them we may give those gents a surprise they won't like. Come on, straight across the prairie to the east till I give the word; then we'll turn south. Ride, and ride fast.'

He sent Shadow through the straggle of brush and racing across the range. Stewart's big roan had speed and Slade had to hold his own mount in but little. A half-mile or so distant from the trail he swerved south.

'I don't think they can spot us at this

distance,' he said. 'Thank Pete, there's no moon.'

'What you aim to do?' jolted Stewart.

'I'll show you when we get there,' Slade answered. 'Ride!'

They rode at top speed. Slade knew the racing horses would out-distance the herd, even though they had to negotiate three sides of the rectangle while the cows followed a straight course. He estimated the distance carefully, waited a little longer, and swerved west. Soon the dark wall of growth flanking the sunken trail came into view. They reached it. The belt was comparatively narrow. Slade pushed well into the outer straggle, pulled up and dismounted. Stewart followed suit.

'Cut brush,' Slade told him. 'The outer branches. It's dry as tinder and will burn like a flash. Pile it right on the lip of the sag. Get busy, we've no time to waste.'

As they worked, he strained his ears to catch the first sound of the approaching herd. They had a sizeable heap of cut branches before he heard the first distant, hoofbeat. He hacked loose a straight limb with a forked end and wedged the spreading fork against the pile of brush.

'Get ready with matches,' he ordered. 'Squat down beside the pile and set it afire when I tell you; then hop back out of the way, get your iron out and be ready to shoot when I do. Okay?'

'Okay,' chuckled Stewart, getting the drift of things. He crouched beside the heap. Slade gripped the end of the forked branch.

Louder and louder sounded the dull roar of approaching hoofs. Slade estimated there were well more than a hundred prime beef critters in the widelooper herd. Louder and louder, a low thunder that vibrated the brush. Slade tensed for action.

'Light it!' he snapped. He saw Stewart scratch a match. There was a tiny flicker, a little spurtle of smoke, pale against the starlight. A crawling flower of fire. Then a roaring flame that shot upward. Stewart leaped back. Slade heaved with his forked branch. Over the lip went the fiercely burning heap.

The result was pandemonium. The terrified cows surged back on their haunches. The leaders whirled and tried to flee, and instantly there was a bawling, clashing tangle. The rustlers, bellowing curses, raced forward and were instantly engulfed by the herd.

Both Slade's guns let go with a rattling crash. His great voice rolled forth.

'Let 'em have it, boys! Don't let one of the skunks get away!'

Stewart was also pulling trigger as fast as he could. It was like shooting at shadows in the lurid and flickering light of the burning brush, but a man toppled from the saddle, clutching at his blood-spurting shoulder.

From beneath the churning hoofs of the maddened cattle came scream after scream of agony and horror. Those awful shrieks from their companion dying in torment frightened the wideloopers more than the banging of the guns. Sheer panic struck them.

'Ride!' howled a voice. 'It's a trap! Ride!'

The horses, as terrified as their masters, tore through the milling cattle, flinging them right and left. Before Slade could reload his empty guns, the last rustler had vanished down the dark tunnel of the gulch. The frantic beat of racing hoofs faded swiftly in the distance.

'Well, I guess that takes care of that,' the ranger remarked, ejecting the spent shells from his guns and replacing them with fresh cartridges.

Old Blaine gulped in his throat, retched frankly. 'I—I feel like being sick,' he gurgled. 'My God, what an awful way to die!'

'Yes, taking the Big Jump under a stampede isn't a nice way to pass on,' Slade agreed. 'He's nothing but bloody pulp, by now. Well, I think we can get down to the trail a little farther on. Might as well shove those cows back where they belong; they're quieting, now.'

Stewart turned his head when they reached the reddened horror that had been a man, but Slade dismounted and by the flicker of the dying flames gazed at what was left of the drygulcher's face. He felt that he should examine the contents of the fellow's pockets,

96

but his stomach turned from the grisly task. To heck with it! He'd learn what he had on him, if anything of importance, which was unlikely, after the sheriff had been notified and the body packed to the coroner. Remounting, he busied himself getting the more than a hundred nervous cows headed back to their home range. And very quickly Blaine Stewart realized what a tophand he had hired. He was shaking his head in wordless admiration by the time the chore was finished and the cows ambling contentedly back the way they had come.'

'Slade,' he said, 'I 'pear to be getting more and more in your debt all the time. You save my carcass from getting an airhole let in it, and you save my cows. I wonder what next?'

'I may ultimately save you from yourself,' Slade replied. 'I hope so.'

'Now what do you mean by that?' demanded the puzzled rancher.

'Perhaps you'll learn later,' Slade replied, and changed the subject. Stewart shook his head again and refrained from asking questions he felt sure would not be answered.

A light burned in the living room when they reached the ranchhouse and they found Ellen sitting up waiting for them.

'Where have you been?' she demanded of her father. 'You said you'd be back early. Do you realize it's nearly daylight?'

'We were sort of—held up,' old Blaine

mumbled. Slade chuckled and she turned on him.

'I thought you'd be a good influence, Mr. Slade, but you're just as bad as he is. I'll expect you to take better care of him in the future.'

'I will, if you'll stop "mistering" me,' he replied. 'I happen to have a first name, and I think you know what it is.'

The dimple showed at the corner of her mouth. 'Okay—Walt,' she said. 'And my friends don't usually call me "Miss Stewart."'

'Can't we have something to eat?' old Blaine asked plaintively. 'I'm starvin'.'

'I'll make you something to eat, but you don't deserve it,' she replied. 'Come along, Walt, and give me a hand.'

In the kitchen, she closed the door and turned to him.

'Now tell me what happened,' she ordered. 'I know something did, it showed in his face.'

Slade told her. She listened in silence and her eyes looked worried.

'I wonder who could have been responsible?' she said.

'I wish I knew for sure,' Slade answered.

'You don't think that—' her voice trailed off.

'No, I don't think the Hargus boys had anything to do with it,' he answered. 'In fact, I'm willing to swear they didn't.'

'The cows would have had to pass over their land to reach the southern trails through the hills to Mexico,' she remarked.

'I've thought of that,' he returned. 'Are there any ways through the western hills?'

'I suppose so,' she replied. 'I recall oldtimers speaking of trails the Indians used, farther to the south. They'd have to cross the Bar M to reach them.'

'The Bar M is the Mason holding, I believe,' Slade observed.

'Yes,' she answered. 'But they'd have had to turn from the Alforki trail to reach the hills. Otherwise they'd run the risk of being seen; the Bar M ranchhouse is close to the trail.'

'I see,' Slade said thoughtfully. 'I'll put some more wood in the stove.'

After they finished eating, Ellen said, 'Now you two head for bed pronto, and I don't want to hear a peep out of either of you before noon.'

Old Blaine obediently stumped up the stairs. Slade insisted on helping her with the dishes, and she didn't object too strongly.

'Now I'm really tired,' she admitted when they returned to the living room. 'I don't believe I've got the strength left to climb the stairs.'

'That's easily taken care of,' Slade chuckled. He picked her up and cradled her in his arms. She smiled and blushed and did not ask to be put down.

At her door he dropped her lightly to her feet. 'That helped a lot,' she said. 'Here's your pay!'

Standing on tip-toe, her lips clung to his a moment. 'Now go to bed,' she whispered. 'The boys will be tumbling out soon, and I hear Charley already stirring. Good night!'

She closed the door, again very softly. Slade entered his own room and sat down for a cigarette before going to sleep. Things appeared to be getting a mite complicated, not unpleasantly.

Ten

Slade had no trouble sleeping till noon. When he awoke with golden sunshine pouring in the window he lay for some minutes in drowsy content, conning over the happenings of the past twenty-four hours. Altogether they were rather satisfactory. He had managed to put Blaine Stewart more under obligation to him and he believed he was strengthening his influence over the stubborn old rancher. He was not at all sure yet that he would be able to change Stewart's attitude toward the rangers, but if he continued to get favorable breaks, he believed there was a chance. So far he wasn't doing so bad. And incidentally, he wasn't doing too bad with Stewart's very charming daughter. He wondered with whom her sympathies would be when the inevitable showdown came.

He took his time dressing and smoked a cigarette before descending the stairs. In the hall he met Blaine rubbing his eyes and still looking sleepy.

'Well, how are my two night hawks?' Ellen greeted them. 'You're making one of me, too; I've been up less than an hour. Dad, I sent Toby to town to notify the sheriff of what happened last night.'

'A good notion,' grunted Stewart. 'He'd oughta know about it. I'm hungry!'

'Your breakfast, if I may call it that, is ready,' she said. 'The boys have already eaten. I told Joe to round up those cows you brought home and shove them back onto their pasture.'

'Good!' said her father. 'Let's eat.'

After breakfast, Slade repaired to the office to finish up the book work. Later, Stewart joined him. He was holding the copy of the *Herald* Hodson Vane had given him the day before.

'Vane's got a hot one in this issue,' he chuckled. 'Here, read it and tell me what you think of it.'

Slade took the paper and perused the article, which began, 'The system is a failure and a disgrace to our State, and should be swept from the statute book without ceremony.'

Followed a tirade of vilification and abuse baked on questionable allegations and half-truths, but written in a singularly smooth and

101

convincing style. It included what Editor Vane was pleased to call a 'Roll of Horror,' the names of men said to have been 'murdered' by the rangers. Among the names, Slade noted more than a few notorious outlaws and killers but who, according to Hodson Vane, were receptacles of all the virtues.

Slade handed the paper back to Stewart without comment. The latter, however, was too busy with his own thoughts to notice the omission.

'That's one of the best yet,' he said pridefully. 'I've got those hellions on the run and I'll soon have 'em corraled and hogtied. For years I've worked and planned and connived and saved money to even up the score for my brother's killing. Now I'm about ready to drop my loop. Wouldn't you say so?'

Slade did not reply at once. He slowly rolled a cigarette with the slim fingers of his left hand and lighted it, his eyes never leaving the rancher's face.

'Mr. Stewart,' he finally asked, 'did you ever see a hog-nosed snake teased?'

Old Blaine's eyes widened and he looked puzzled. 'Why, no, I never did,' he replied. 'What about it?'

'Old Hog-nose,' Slade began reminiscently, 'is a rather tough looking jigger; and when he fills himself with air and flattens his head and spreads his hood to almost three times the normal size, just like the deadly cobra, he looks even tougher. But really he is a harmless critter, gentle and timid. All he wants to do is slip away and hide. But get him cornered so he can't get away, he rolls over on his back and plays dead. Plays it so well you can handle him without his showing a sign of life. He puts on a real show.

'The only flaw in the show is that he's learned his lesson too darn well. Turn him onto his belly and he'll immediately roll over on his back again. That's the position a dead snake is supposed to assume and he insists on playing the game according to the rules. But if you keep turning him over so that he has to flop back again and again, he begins to get mad. Finally he gets really mad. And what does he do? He flops around and bites himself. He hasn't any venom, but he does have large fangs in his rear jaw. He is an example of the rear-fanged snakes which are the link between the non-venomous and the venomous serpents that have their "hypodermic" fangs in front. He uses those fangs to puncture the bodies of frogs which resist being swallowed by inhaling deeply and puffing up. Those fangs can inflict a pretty hefty bite.

'Yes, he bites himself, his anger turning against himself, spoiling his disposition and his health, for if he's teased long enough, the poor devil will eventually bite himself to death.'

Slade paused, took a puff on his cigarette,

glanced out the window. Old Blaine looked still more puzzled, but expectant.

'Mr. Stewart,' Slade resumed, 'that's a fair notion of what happens to a man who holds a grudge, who nurses the desire for vengeance in his heart; all the time he's "biting" himself. Vengeance! "Revenge, at first though sweet, Bitter ere long back on itself recoils." It embitters a man, poisons his nature, ruins his happiness.'

For a full moment, old Blaine did not speak, then he shook his head in a resigned gesture.

'Slade,' he sighed, 'sometimes I wish I hadn't ever taken the trouble to find you. Dadblast it! You get me all mixed up, and bothered. I hardly know what you're talking about, but it bothers me. Why can't you leave me in peace?'

'Mr. Stewart,' Slade said gently, 'how long has it been since you really knew peace?'

Blaine Stewart sighed again, heavily. 'I don't know,' he answered. 'I really don't know. Oh, the devil! I'm going for a ride. Go talk with Ellen; she'll be a match for you.'

He rose to his feet and stamped out of the office. Slade gazed after him, his eyes compassionate. Then he turned and went back to work on the books.

It was Ellen who came to him. She walked into the office and laid a hand on his shoulder.

'What did you do to him?' she demanded.

'Who?' Slade asked, turning around,

although he knew very well whom she meant.

'My father,' she replied. 'You must have disturbed him quite a good deal to make him cross with me. You didn't quarrel with him, did you? Nobody ever dares quarrel with him.'

'No, I didn't quarrel with him,' Slade answered. 'And, which is more important, he didn't quarrel with me.'

'Well, you did something to him,' she insisted. 'He really oughtn't to be upset like that. I'm beginning to fear you are a rather terrible person, even though you seem so nice.'

Slade gently drew her down on his knee and cupped her chin in his hand. Her wide eyes looked up into his and her color rose.

'Honey,' he said, 'I wish only the best of everything for your father. I'm sorry if I upset him, but anything I may say to him is for his own good. Which I am sure he will himself acknowledge after reflection and his better judgment takes over.'

'I believe you,' she replied, her voice a little tremulous. 'Poor old Dad! As I said to you before, he is not a happy man. Sometimes I fear he never will be.'

'In that I think you're wrong,' he said. 'I've a strong notion that before everything is finished, he'll be happy, and—content.'

He leaned over and kissed her lightly on the lips. 'Now trot along and let me finish my work,' he said. 'I'll talk to you later.'

'And maybe you'll sing for us this evening,'

she insinuated.

'Yes, I will, if you really wish me to,' he promised.

Old Blaine got back from his ride around dark. He was in a better temper and hungry. Slade and Ellen had already eaten with the hands, a happy-go-lucky bunch, mostly young, whom Slade liked at once, but they sat with him through his dinner.

'Your books are all straightened out,' Slade told him. 'Tomorrow I'll head out on the range.'

'Tomorrow you'll take it easy,' Stewart corrected. 'After that chore you must be tuckered. Take tomorrow off.'

'And perhaps you'll take me for a ride,' Ellen added.

'That would be a pleasure,' Slade smilingly replied.

'And now you're going to sing for us—you promised,' Ellen said when they repaired to the living room. 'You play the piano, of course?'

Slade nodded.

'I had that music box sent all the way from Dallas for Ellen,' Stewart observed. 'The best money could buy. I play some myself. I only use one finger, but I can make her hum.'

Ellen shuddered and raised her eyes to heaven.

'Uh huh, you can make her hum all right,' old Charley, who had drifted in from the kitchen, snorted sarcastically. 'Sounds like half a dozen skeletons dancing on a tin roof!'

'Please, Walt,' Ellen begged. 'Don't pay any attention to them.'

Slade sang for them. Old Blaine was so enthusiastic that he insisted on calling all the hands and crowding them into the room to hear.

'Makes a feller feel like he wants to give up all his bad habits and live a plumb virtuous life,' observed saturnine Joe Callison, the range boss.

'If that's so where you're concerned, the day of miracles is at hand,' Stewart declared positively. 'Give us another, Slade.'

'Makes me feel just the opposite,' Ellen whispered, with a giggle. Much later she reminded him, 'You promised to take me riding.'

'If you don't get some sleep you won't be able to ride,' he retorted. 'Haven't you any idea what time it is!'

*   *   *

Nevertheless, two hours before noon found them riding south. Slade was impressed by the excellence of the range and the fine condition of the cows grazing on the lush grass. No matter what else he might be, Blaine Stewart was a cattleman.

'We're passing over the Mason holding now,' Ellen observed some time later. 'It's long and narrow; their cows and ours intermingle a good deal and have to be cut out at roundup time.'

Slade nodded absently. He was studying the western hills, which were heavily brush-grown, especially at the base. Far up one long slope he noted an indenture in the chaparral that wound upward to the distant crest.

'That's a trail up there, sure as shooting,' he mused. 'Wonder how in blazes you get to it?'

Passing the Mason spread they rode on through a day of sunshine and balmy breezes. The Big Bend was showing what it could do weatherwise, and when in a beneficent mood it's hard to beat.

'We're approaching the Bradded H, the Hargus ranch,' she finally told him. 'Shall we turn back, or keep on going?'

'Don't see any reason why we shouldn't keep on going,' he replied. 'Don't see any "Keep Off" signs. Only I expect your father wouldn't exactly approve.'

'*Qjos que no ven, corazon que no ilora*,' she quoted.

'If the eyes do not see, the heart does not grieve,' he translated with a chuckle. 'But is that just exactly fair?'

'He can do his grieving after I tell him, which will be as soon as we get back to the spread,' she replied. 'I can handle him.'

Which Slade did not in the least doubt.

So they rode on across the Bradded H

range. Once or twice they saw Bradded H cowboys going about their chores. These waved to them but did not approach.

'I used to visit down here quite frequently before old Conrad Withrow died,' Ellen said. 'Dad always wanted this property, but when Uncle Conrad died, his sister in Corpus Cristi inherited the ranch. She knew the Hargus boys and sold to them before Dad could contact her. He was rather miffed about it, and he and the Harguses never could get along. I was away at school when Joe Callison had the trouble with young Tom. If I'd been home then, the chances are I could have persuaded Dad not to press a charge against Tom Hargus. I don't have any patience with his silly quarrels with his neighbors.'

Slade nodded gravely; he began to believe he could count on her support when the showdown came.

Eleven

The sun was low in the west as they neared the old ranchhouse with its whispering pines and its hillside graves. Standing in the yard was a tall and stalwart figure gazing into the blaze of the sunset, the reddish rays illuminating his rugged face.

'There's Andy now,' Slade observed.

Ellen gazed at the brooding figure. 'What a splendid looking man he is,' she said.

'And I've a notion he's just as splendid as he looks,' Slade observed.

She slanted him a glance through her lashes. 'Do you recall what Priscilla said to John Alden in Longfellow's poem, "Miles Standish"?' she asked.

Slade chuckled. ' "Speak for yourself, John," I believe it was,' he replied, adding innocently, 'Why?'

Ellen shrugged daintily. 'I'll let you find the answer,' she said.

Slade chuckled again. 'But John Alden was a steady-going young man with prospects, not a homeless wanderer,' he pointed out.

Miss Stewart's answer was an undignified sniff.

Andy Hargus turned at the sound of hoofs. An expression of astonishment bordering on disbelief crossed his craggy features. However, he quickly recovered his aplomb and came forward with great lithe strides, hand out-stretched, his teeth shining white in a smile.

'Well, this is a surprise!' he exclaimed.

'Hope it's not an unpleasant one,' Slade replied. 'We were riding this way and thought we'd drop in on you.'

'It's sure anything but unpleasant,' Andy declared heartily. 'Light off and come in. I'm mighty, mighty glad to see you both.'

His eyes were on Ellen's face as he said it.

Slade repressed a grin. He repressed another one when Hargus hurried to help Ellen to dismount. He dropped back a pace as they headed for the ranchhouse.

"When they entered, they saw that Hargus already had a visitor. Clyde Hartsook, the former member of the Brocius gang and the leader of the east valley faction, was sitting by a window smoking. He rose to his feet, nodded cordially to Slade and bowed to Ellen.

Hargus performed the introduction. Hartsook bowed again and turned back to the window.

Ellen glanced around the room. 'You've sure made some changes in the old place, Mr. Hargus, and for the better,' she commented.

'Would you like to see the new barn and what I've done to the bunkhouse and other buildings?' Hargus asked eagerly.

'I would,' she replied. 'Show me, please.'

They left the room together. 'See you later, gentlemen,' Ellen said, slanting a sideways glance at Slade. Hartsook's cold, dead-looking eyes followed them.

'Guess she's not much like her old man,' he remarked to Slade.

'I think that at the bottom he's a good deal like her,' the ranger replied.

'Maybe,' Hartsook conceded, 'but he sure don't show it.' Abruptly he turned to face Slade.

'Heard from old Wyatt Earp recently?' he

asked. Slade dissembled his surprise. 'Why, no, not lately,' he answered.

'Understand he's making a pile out of oil lands in California,' Hartsook observed. 'I always liked Wyatt, though we were sort of on different sides of the corral bars. He's an honest man. Just as I believe Blaine Stewart is an honest man, even though he does feel the world needs making over and he's the jigger to do it. I was in Tombstone when you were there and saved Earp from getting his comeuppance. Oh, don't worry about me shooting my mouth off. I know how to keep a tight latigo on my jaw. In the business I was in for quite a few years you learn to, or you don't last long. When you're ready to let folks know what you are and why you're here, I reckon you will. But that's your business, none of mine.'

'Thank you,' Slade said. Hartsook nodded.

'There's another feller here who was in Tombstone when I was there, and I've kept my mouth shut about him,' Hartsook resumed.

'Yes?' Slade prompted.

'Yes, that feller Hodson Vane who puts out old Stewart's newspaper. He was dealing cards in the Crystal Palace Saloon in Tombstone when I was hanging out there.'

'And turns up here an editor,' Slade commented.

'Oh, he's a newspaper man, all right, and a good one,' Hartsook replied. 'Him and John Ringo—you remember Ringo, of course—

were quite chummy and John told me considerable about him. He had a prime job on a big daily back East but got fired for some kind of skullduggery and drifted west. Reckon when a feller really has larceny in his system it stays there. He gambled a lot while he was in Tombstone and did mighty well at it—made a pile. Did too darn well, some folks began to think, so Vane trailed his twine while he was still in one piece. Went to Dallas. Understand he bought a little spread with his winnings and got a job on a newspaper there. That's where old Stewart met him and hired him. He's smart, all right, mighty smart, as Stewart is liable to find out before he's finished with him. He's kind of chummy with the Mason brothers.'

'Know anything about the Masons?' Slade asked. Hartsook shook his head.

'Not much, and I don't want to know anything about them,' he disclaimed.

'Why?'

'Because I ain't got no use for card sharps, and that's what Wes Mason is,' Hartsook answered. 'He had poor Tom Hargus head over heels in debt to him before Tom got sent to the pen. Andy and Hank didn't know about it. Reckon they still don't know. No, I haven't any use for the Mason sort. I busted the law plenty in my time, but I did it with a gun against other jiggers with guns, and took my chances. I don't cotton to the kind of hellions

113

who have a smile for your face and a knife for your back. Yes, I busted the law when I was young and wild, but that's past and done for now. Well, here comes Andy and the gal, and I've got to be riding. Be seeing you.'

'Hartsook,' Slade asked, 'why have you been telling me what you have?'

'Because I figure you for a squareshooter who's trying to do an honest job, and I do cotton to that sort,' the rancher answered over his shoulder as he walked out, leaving Slade pondering the unusual character that was Clyde Hartsook.

However, he quickly dismissed Hartsook himself from his thoughts, but he did not dismiss what Hartsook told him.

Ellen and Andy Hargus entered the room. 'Yes, we'll have a cup of coffee and a sandwich with you, but no more,' she was saying. 'We must be leaving soon. It will be very late when we get home as it is, and I don't want Dad to worry.'

'You'll come again?' Hargus asked eagerly.

'Yes, we will,' Ellen replied. 'I've enjoyed our visit very much.'

As they rode north under the last glow of sunset, Slade turned to his companion.

'Well, what do you think of him?' he asked.

'I like him,' she returned frankly. 'I think he has the makings of a fine man.'

'He has,' Slade agreed. 'All he needs is a good woman to keep her thumb down on him, hard.'

'A good woman?'

'Well, a nice and charming one,' he chuckled.

It was late when they reached the Slash S ranchhouse. Old Blaine was sitting up in the living room.

'About time you got home,' he growled. 'I'm hungry.'

'Did you think Walt had run off to Mexico with me?' Ellen asked gaily, rumpling his hair.

'Guess worse things could happen,' her father replied composedly. 'But he'd bring you back when he found out about that dratted temper you have. For the life of me, I can't understand where you got it from. Let's eat!'

*　　　*　　　*

A quiet week followed. Slade rode the range with the other hands and quickly gained their admiration and respect.

'He's one of the natural-born cowmen sort you run into about once in a lifetime,' said taciturn, fault-finding Joe Callison, the range boss. 'He always knows the right thing to do, and does it. I wish I had about fifty of the same kind. I'd set back in an easy chair and never have to bother my head about anything.'

'You're getting to be not so much of a blasted fool as I've always had you branded,' Charley Simpson, the irascible cook, told him.

115

'Anyhow it looks like you know a real hand when you see one. Even Blaine's been showing some signs of intelligence since he landed here. Maybe good sense is catchin', like the itch.'

Slade also found opportunity a couple of times to ride south to the Bar M holding and study the slopes of the western hills. More than ever he was convinced that a trail ran up those slopes, although where it reached the level ground, if it did, was not apparent. However, being familiar with such tracks, he felt confident that he could locate where it began at the base of the hills, if occasion to do so warranted a search for it.

There was always plenty of book work to do and Slade spent considerable time in the office. He had just finished a chore of going over accounts and had joined old Blaine in the living room when there was a clatter of hoofs outside followed by a babble of excited voices. A cowboy dashed into the room, his face working, his eyes dilated, gibbering unintelligible speech.

'What in blazes!' shouted Stewart, jumping up from his chair. The hand mouthed incoherent words.

With a long stride, Slade was beside him. He gripped the wildly excited man by the shoulder and shook him vigorously.

'Get hold of yourself, feller!' he snapped. 'What's the matter? What's happened?'

'It's Joe,' gabbled the cowboy, calming a little. 'We've got him outside, what's left of him. He's dead!'

Old Blaine gave a roar of anguish. 'Tobe, you don't mean it!'

'Yes, I do,' replied the cowboy as Slade's grip tightened on his shoulder. 'We found him down on the south pasture—shot in the back!'

Twelve

Bellowing curses, Stewart stormed from the house. Slade let go the cowboy's bruised shoulder, sat down and began rolling a cigarette with steady fingers.

Old Blaine returned. His face was flushed and working, there was a mad sparkle in his eyes and he weaved slightly on his feet.

'This settles it!' he said thickly. 'This settles it!'

'Mr. Stewart,' Slade said, 'sit down and cool off before something bad happens to you. Sit down, I say!'

Old Blaine started as if awakening suddenly from a bad dream. He stared at Slade, unseeingly, and slumped into a chair.

'This settles it,' he repeated. 'I'm going to get the boys together and ride down and clean out that nest of snakes once for all.'

'Who?' Slade asked.

'The blankety-blanked Harguses, that's who!' Stewart stormed.

'Mr. Stewart,' Slade said, intent on changing the course of the rancher's thoughts, 'what did Charley, the old cook, call you?'

Stewart's eyes widened and he looked bewildered. 'Why—why he called me a blasted fool,' he replied.

'Are you going to prove him right?' Slade asked. 'If you attack the Harguses, it will very likely be your finish. There are some two hundred men over in the east valley who have little love for you, and they do like the Harguses. Attempt what you just threatened and you'll quite probably end up the prime attraction of a necktie party, after they've done for the rest of us.'

Stewart started to answer, but Slade forestalled him. 'Mr. Stewart,' he said, 'do the Harguses strike you as the sort of men who would shoot somebody in the back?'

Blaine hemmed and hawed and ended sputtering.

'Well, do they?' Slade persisted.

'No,' the rancher was forced to admit.

'They are not,' Slade said flatly. 'The night of the ruckus in the sheriff's office, if you'd turned your back on Andy Hargus and walked out, all he'd have done would have been to dance up and down in futile anger and bawl to you to come back and fight like a man. You know it as well as I do.'

'But if it wasn't the Harguses, who was it?' Stewart demanded. 'Some hellion from the east valley?'

'Highly improbable,' Slade replied. 'They had nothing against Callison over there. They don't take kindly to your overlord attitude but I doubt if there's a man there who would even think of doing you bodily harm, without extreme provocation.'

'Then who in the blankety blue blazes murdered poor Joe?' the rancher wailed.

'I don't know, yet, but I expect to find out,' Slade said quietly.

Stewart glanced at him, and shrank a little in his chair. For suddenly he was looking into the terrible eyes of *El Halcon*, glacier-cold, with little smoky flames flickering in their depths. Living eyes in a face of death. Old Blaine Stewart never forgot that look in Walt Slade's eyes; he turned away from it.

'What next!' he mumbled. 'What next!'

'I can tell you with great certainty, sir, if you don't do exactly as I say,' Slade said. 'Quite probably you are next.'

Stewart blinked. 'What do you mean?' he asked.

'I mean, in the words of an old proverb, that you have sowed the wind and now you are reaping the whirlwind. You have unwittingly played into the hands of certain unscrupulous and utterly ruthless men with ends of their own to further, and to further which your

119

death is necessary. In my opinion, murdering Joe Callison was their last attempt to get you embroiled in a fight with the Harguses, in which you'd eventually be killed. When they learn that attempt has failed, they are liable to resort to direct methods. I repeat, if you value your life, listen to me. I've had dealings with such men and know how they think and act. Listen to me, and do exactly what I tell you to do.'

'He will,' broke in Ellen, who had entered the room a few minutes before to stand listening. 'Do you hear, Dad? You'll do exactly what Walt tells you.'

'All right,' Stewart groaned. 'I can't think for myself. I believe I'm going mad. For God's sake, get me a drink!'

Slade nodded and Ellen hurried to fetch it. Stewart gulped the whiskey like water.

'And now some coffee,' Slade whispered to the girl. 'We've got to get him quieted down or he is liable to have a stroke of some sort. He looks to be on the verge of one.'

Stewart's rage seemed to have cooled and was replaced with a numb apathy. He sat staring straight ahead, muttering under his breath, shaking his head now and then, uncertainly.

Charley came in bringing the coffee, concern written large on his wrinkled face.

'Here's your coffee, Blaine, steaming hot, drink it down now like a good boy and I'll get you some more,' he said as gently and persuasively as if he were addressing the little tad that sixty years before he had walloped for his own good.

Stewart obediently sipped the coffee until the cup was empty. Charley hurried out for more.

Gradually Stewart began to brighten a bit as the whiskey and the hot coffee soothed his tortured nerves.

'Guess I'll have to appoint somebody range boss,' he remarked.

'Reckon you won't have to look far,' said Charley as he entered with the refilled cup.

'Guess I won't,' Stewart agreed. 'Slade, you'll have to take over. There's nobody else I can really trust to handle the chore as it should be handled. I don't know what I'd do without you. I hope you'll never leave me.'

He glanced at his daughter, who smiled wistfully.

'And now what is it you have to tell me?' he asked.

'First,' Slade said, 'never ride alone until I tell you that you can. Always have one of the boys with you; two or three would be better. Never be in town alone. And never sit next to windows after dark. The more you stick around the ranchhouse for a while, the better.'

Stewart nodded, 'I'll do as you say,' he promised. 'I don't think I'm exactly the scary sort, but I'll admit the way you talk you've got me a bit jumpy.'

'Walt,' Ellen put in with a woman's intuition, 'don't you think those warnings apply to you as well?'

Slade shrugged his broad shoulders. 'I've had experience with those kinds of devils, which makes a difference,' he pointed out. Ellen did not look convinced, and did look worried.

'First off I guess you'd better send somebody to town to notify the sheriff, and have them get word to the Reverend up at Marfa that we'll have another chore for him down here in the Valley day after tomorrow,' Stewart said sadly. 'And tell the boys to lay poor Joe out in the room beside the office.'

Slade nodded and left the room to take care of his first chores as range boss.

'I'll give Charley a hand in the kitchen,' Ellen told her father. 'The boys have to eat.'

'Yes, things have to keep moving,' old Blaine agreed. 'You can't stop living just because somebody has passed on. That's one of the hard things of living.'

Sheriff Dave Barnes and Doc Cooper rode to the ranch-house and held an inquest. The same dreary verdict as that which was registered on young Tom Hargus was returned: 'Death at the hands of a party or parties unknown.'

After the inquest, Sheriff Barnes talked with Stewart, alone. 'I'm doing the best I can,

Blaine, but I don't seem to have much luck with such cases,' he told the rancher. 'After all, I'm no range detective, I'm just a former cowhand who got elected, largely by your help.'

'I know it, Dave,' Stewart returned heavily. 'I know you'll do all you can.' He paused. 'Slade said that I'm next, if I don't watch my step.'

'He could be right,' the sheriff conceded. 'Things seem to be going from bad to worse.' He also paused. It took courage for even Dave Barnes to make the suggestion he offered.

'Blaine,' he said, 'maybe you ought to send for the rangers.'

Stewart did not explode, as the sheriff fully expected he would. He merely shook his head.

'Slade said he expected to find out who killed Joe,' he observed with apparent irrelevance.

'*El Halcon*'s got a reputation for that sort of thing,' the sheriff replied.

'I got a look at his eyes when he said it,' Stewart went on. 'Dave, they scared me. I never saw such a look in a man's eyes. I'd rather face the Devil himself than Walt Slade with that look in his eyes. It gave me the creeps.'

'He's a strange young feller,' admitted the sheriff. 'I don't understand him. I hope you'll be able to keep him here and settle him down before he gets into real trouble some time.'

'I don't think he ever will,' Stewart said. 'But

123

I sure would like to keep him here. I don't know, though. *El Halcon*! The Hawk! The name fits. That's what he's like, one of those big, ice-eyed devils of the mountains that's scared of nothing and can give an eagle his comeuppance. You can't cage that sort.'

Several cowboys sat the death watch over Joe Callison during the night. Slade and Stewart remained in the big living room, with Ellen flitting in and out from the kitchen and the room where Callison's body lay in the coffin that had hurriedly been dispatched from Alforki. The old rancher was strangely subdued and sat silent for the most part, occupied with his gloomy thoughts.

'Slade,' he said suddenly, 'I wonder if I did Tom Hargus an injustice when I pushed that charge against him last year?'

'Yes, I think you did,' Slade replied. 'Unintentionally, I'll grant, but you did.'

'I'm afraid you're right,' Stewart said heavily. Slade felt that it took considerable for him to say what he said next.

'I wonder,' he remarked, 'is there any way I could make amends?'

'I think there is,' Slade answered. 'You might send the Hargus brothers an invitation to attend Callison's funeral.'

Stewart looked a bit startled. 'I'm—I'm afraid they wouldn't accept it,' he demurred.

'I think they would,' Slade replied. 'I think they would be glad to. Especially if your

124

daughter brought it to them. Send her down there with a couple of the boys and see what happens.'

'Dad, I'd be glad to,' Ellen, who had entered the room at that moment, said. 'I think Walt is right, and I'm sure Mr. Hargus would accept.'

'All right,' Stewart said wearily. 'Have it your way. I hope you two don't mind, but I'm going upstairs to lay down a while; I feel tuckered.'

'An excellent idea,' Slade agreed. 'You've had a bad day.'

Ellen Stewart did make the trip to the Bradded H spread the following day, and on the afternoon of the funeral the many townspeople and others who came to pay their last respects to Joe Callison were vastly astonished to see the Hargus brothers standing with the Stewarts, father and daughter.

Once again Walt Slade stood beside an open grave. All was in readiness. Only the appearance of the minister was awaited.

Suddenly a cowhand on a lathered horse came pounding up the trail. He dismounted and hurried to where old Blaine was standing.

'Mr. Stewart,' he said, 'the Reverend can't make it; he's sick in bed. Had a stroke or something this morning.'

A blank expression, tinged with sorrow, overspread the rancher's face.

'I just can't bear to see Joe put away without something being said over him,' he muttered.

Abruptly his face brightened. He turned to his tall range boss.

'Slade,' he said, 'couldn't you sort of say the service over Joe?'

'I'll try, from memory,' Slade acceded. 'I've heard the service read quite a few times.'

He stepped forward, bowed his black head and raised his hand. After the moment of silent prayer, his rich, deep voice spoke the service, word for word, even as the old minister read it over Tom Hargus' remains.

A hush fell over the gathering, a hush that deepened as the last inspired words rose calm and clear over the soft thud of the falling earth:

'"From the voiceless lips of the unreplying dead there comes no word, but in the night of death, Hope sees a star, and listening Love can hear the rustle of a wing!"'

A deep sigh arose as Slade stepped back and the grave was mounded over. A white-haired old storekeeper remarked to a friend, 'There are folks who say that young feller is an owlhoot, but I've got a feeling that when he talks to God—God listens!'

Thirteen

A pall hung over the Slash S for a few days, but only a few. Death, sharp and sudden, is a too frequent occurrence on the range for a very lasting impression to be made. Very quickly things were back to normal. Slade prescribed the panacea of hard work, and did not spare himself.

'He's a cowman,' one of the older hands told Blaine Stewart. 'He's a driver, too, but he doesn't ask anybody to tackle something he won't tackle himself. Fact is, if the chore is really a tough one, he takes over. And the boys all like him, too. He can look at you and make you squirm, and he can look at you and make you feel good all over. Yep, he's okay; hope he'll stay with us.'

With the ranch again functioning smoothly, Slade found time for an exploration he had contemplated ever since he and Ellen Stewart rode to the Hargus spread. He headed south to the Mason holding, only this time he did not follow the Alforki trail, by a branch of which they had reached the Bradded H ranchhouse, but rode to the west along the base of the hills until he neared the point where he saw the peculiar indenture crawling up the slopes and marking, he believed, the course of an old Indian trail.

He was not forking Shadow, for he seldom risked the great black's legs in ranch work, but the tall roan Blaine Stewart rode the night they had the brush with the rustlers. The roan was not Shadow, but he was an excellent work horse endowed with endurance and good speed.

'Feller,' Slade told him, 'we're getting close to where I figure that snake track up there should slide down to the level ground. The brush grows thick down here at the foot of the slopes, but where that trail opens up it should be somewhat thinner, and I've a notion we'll find signs that'll tell us it's been used fairly recently. So keep your eyes skinned, horse, and let me know if I miss anything.'

The roan snorted and Slade rode on, scanning the bristle of growth with eyes that missed nothing.

'Here it is!' he suddenly exclaimed. 'See where the twigs are broken and the leaves withered, with the branches sort of pushed back sideways? Something has gone through there, horse, and not long ago. Okay, here we go, don't mind the thorns; if I can take it, so can you.'

The roan shoved his way into the chaparral, which here was, as his rider predicted, quite a bit thinner.

Intent on his hoped-for discovery, Slade had been paying scant heed to his surroundings. So he did not spot the horseman who sat his mount on a fairly distant rise at the edge of a clump of thicket with which he blended. Nor did he see the rider turn his horse and ride south at a fast pace. For before that happened he was through the light screen of chaparral and the roan's irons were ringing on the hard surface of the trail Slade had felt sure would reach the level ground at this spot.

The trail, broad enough for three men to ride abreast, was in the nature of a wide ditch, its surface, hard almost as stone, was more than a foot below the level of the ground on either side. The thick vegetation of the encroaching growth met overhead, interlacing into a natural pergola through which the rays of the sun filtered in a golden twilight. On its surface there was practically no growth.

'It was beaten down by a myriad of moccasined feet in the course of untold centuries,' Slade explained to the roan. 'Beaten so hard and compact that rain water does not penetrate the surface and the earth below has become dessicated and salty, so that nothing will grow. Down at the edge of the rangeland it very likely branched in various directions and was never beaten down so hard. Grass covered it there and eroded earth provided soil to sustain the growth. I've seen similar phenomena before; they're not infrequent in the hill country where the Indians used to prowl. This one is more pronounced than usual, that is all. So we'll just amble along and see where it leads to. I'm beginning to get a notion about quite a few things that heretofore have been puzzling.'

For nearly a mile he made his way up the tunnel of hazy green sunshine. Then the growth thinned somewhat so that he could glimpse patches of blue sky. It thinned still more as he proceeded and finally sunlight poured down and the brush-walled depression became uncomfortably hot.

Slade rode quite slowly, scanning the growth on either side, for he did not want to miss spotting possible brush-grown off-shoots. He had a pretty definite idea as to where the trail, or a fork, ultimately led and was anxious to put it to the test.

Up and up wound the old track. Slade noted with satisfaction indubitable indications that horses and many cattle had passed that way, some no great time before. Ultimately the track reached the crest of the hills and after a bit abandoned its westerly course and veered south. Slade rode even more slowly, for here there was greater liability of a fork, either branch of which might be the main trail that by now he was convinced led eventually to the Rio Grande and Mexico.

'And very likely to be a straight shoot,' he told the roan. 'I've a notion this was one of the tracks by which the Indians raided into Mexico. The Comanches called September "the Mexican moon," for regularly in that

130

month they came down from their strongholds for an invasion beyond the Rio Grande. Yes, I'm pretty sure this was one of their routes; and very convenient for gents who know about it and hanker to run a few "wet" cows to *manana* land.'

Slade had been so engrossed in his discovery that he had thought for nothing else. It was the pricking of the roan's ears and the backward slant of its head that warned him. Instantly every sense was alert, and to his ears came the clicking of fast hoofs on the trail behind. He turned and looked back.

Around a bend bulged half a dozen riders. They raised a shout as they spotted him. There was no doubt in Slade's mind as to what that exultant yell meant. He spoke to the roan urgently. The big horse scudded ahead, and the race was on.

It was a gruelling race, and Slade quickly realized that he was on the losing end. The roan was not Shadow, who would easily have shown a clean pair of heels to the pursuit. The roan was giving its best, but it wasn't quite enough. He lost a few yards in every hundred. Which meant there could be but one result. Rifles cracked, but the distance was still great for anything like accurate shooting from the back of a moving horse and none of the bullets found a mark. Slade leaned low in the saddle, urging the roan to greater efforts.

The roan proved to be a 'stampeder,' a

131

horse easily frightened, and with that pandemonium behind him he needed no stimulus to get every iota of speed of which he was capable out of him. But steadily the pursuit closed the gap.

Slade eyed the wall of growth; nowhere did he see a spot where he could turn off. Nevertheless, he was contemplating a side dash into the almost impenetrable and thorny tangle when the trail forked, one branch veering slightly to the west, the other and broader trending due south. Slade's hand tightened on the reins; he had to make a decision, with no time for leisurely contemplation. He chose the southerly branch.

In doing which, *El Halcon* made his second mistake of the day.

Swiftly the track grew rougher, scoured by rain water, littered with stones, and Slade realized that it was not the old Indian trail with its almost adamantine surface but an offshoot that might lead anywhere.

A moment later it led into a narrow, brush-choked canyon with sheer side walls, and from which flowed a sizeable stream. Ahead sounded a low rumbling, which meant, he knew, that the gorge was very likely a box and that the stream rushed over a cliff to form a fall. And the going steadily got worse.

The roan was no rock horse and he skated and floundered, losing speed. And now slugs were coming close. The roar of the fall sounded louder, and the hoofbeats of the pursuers also loudened. Slade decided desperate remedies were in order. He slid his Winchester from the saddle boot, gripped the reins with an iron hand, bringing the horse to a sliding halt and whirling him around. The rifle leaped to his shoulder. Fire spurted from the muzzle.

The pursuit was thrown into momentary confusion by the unexpected move. A man fell, then a horse. Another plunged over it. The other riders tried to veer around the wild tangle but were forced to pull up. Slade emptied the magazine as fast as he could pull trigger. He saw a second man reel in the saddle. He jerked his horse's head around to make the most of the temporary advantage. Slugs were coming close.

The roan screamed and reared high. Slade had barely time to kick his feet free from the stirrups and hurl himself sideways before the roan fell, kicking in its death agonies among the stones.

Bruised, battered, the ranger scrambled to his feet, picked up his fallen rifle and fled up the canyon on foot. Behind sounded triumphant whoops and a renewed clattering of hoofs.

As he ran, he stuffed cartridges into the rifle magazine. Very likely they would corner him sooner or later, but he grimly resolved to take as much toll as possible before he was downed.

A little more and he would try worming into the brush to make a last desperate stand.

The roar of the fall was loud now; the canyon evidently shallow. He reached a bend, slewed around and fired a blast at the charging horsemen. A yell of pain and anger echoed the shots. He was throwing off the effects of the fall and his hand was steadier. Whirling, he raced on, with the roar of the falling water but a short distance ahead.

Gradually it dawned on him that there were no further sounds of pursuit behind him. He slackened his speed a little to listen the better. Only the boom of the fall and the soughing of a brisk wind that blew up the canyon greeted his ears. What were the devils up to? Slade began to grow acutely uneasy. That continued silence was ominous. Or had they given up the pursuit? He thought it highly unlikely; they still outnumbered him at least four to one and could easily surround him sooner or later.

He rounded another bend and saw the falls, a scintillating torrent rushing over the end wall of the canyon; and on all three sides the cliffs were sheer, with the dense chaparral growing clear to their base.

There were rocks near the end wall, isolated boulders, and Slade made for them. Soon he was holed up behind one, his eyes fixed on the trail.

But nothing moved there, nor was any sound save the thunder of the fall to be heard.

134

The trail stretched silent and deserted. He searched the brush with his eyes, watching for any abrupt swaying of the upper branches that would denote somebody shoving his way through the close growing trunks. Only the bend of the foliage before the steady blast of air sucking up the canyon was to be seen. He relaxed a little; began to look like the hellions had given up the chase. Perhaps he had inflicted heavier loss on them than he thought. He was pretty sure he had nicked a couple besides the man who fell from his saddle. Could have been more than nicks.

As he gazed down the canyon, it seemed to him the air was growing misty, although the sunshine poured down as bright as ever. He blinked his eyes, thinking he was suffering from an optical illusion; but the grayish haze persisted, even grew thicker. Then into the sky spiraled a bluish column that bent before the force of the wind. The 'mist' was not a mist, nor was it haze. It was smoke!

There could be no doubt of it; the devils had fired the brush and the flames were steadily eating their way up-canyon. Now he could see sparks and burning brands swirling upward on the wings of the wind, glittering palely in the sunlight. Before the fierce current of air the fire was fairly leaping ahead.

For a moment sheer panic threatened to engulf him. Walt Slade had never been afraid to die, but this was a way of dying to shake the nerve of the most fearless. He glared about, seeking some avenue of escape, and found none. The cliffs were sheer. The thick chaparral brushed their rocky sides. A few more minutes and the entire gorge would be a seething inferno in which nothing could live. The poor roan had been lucky. At least his end had been swift and merciful, far better than death by suffocation or fire.

Already the air was growing unbearably hot, and dark with smoke. Slade began to cough, and to gasp for breath. All around him was smoke, falling ash and blistering heat. The water alone looked cool and inviting, rushing unconcernedly down the end wall, although in the lower canyon it must now be scalding hot. Nothing cool and untainted but the fall.

The fall! Abruptly remembrance of certain geological facts pertaining to waterfalls flooded his mind. There might be a chance of escape. That downward rushing column might prove his salvation. A last desperate expedient, but worth trying. After all, he certainly had nothing to lose. If he remained where he was within a few more minutes he would either be suffocated or burned to a crisp.

Clutching his rifle, he slipped from behind the rock and, choking and gasping, scrambled up a little slope to the misty edge of the fall and flattened himself against the cliff. Another instant and, if his surmise was incorrect, he would be plunged into the catch basin and quickly pounded to death against the rocks by the tons of hurtling water.

Hesitating an instant, he took a deep breath of the smoky air, hugged the cliff and stepped boldly into the edge of the fall. For a moment he took a terrific beating from the descending flood; but as he edged along against the rock wall it quickly thinned. Another stride and he found himself in a shallow hollow back of the fall, a condition almost universally prevalent to waterfalls. Scant inches before his face was the steady, scintillating liquid curtain, with overhead the constantly overturning dome of the fall.

The air was thick with water vapor, but it was breathable, much more breathable than that filled with smoke and ash in the canyon outside. He sagged against the wet wall of rock and felt the strength that had been draining from his body renewed.

The water curtain before his eyes was pellucid, green as the edge of an iceberg, seemingly motionless as a sheet of glass, shot through with strange tints born of the sunlight. But as he gazed at its limpid surface it began to change and become charged with a marvelous, ever-changing kaleidoscope of exquisite color. All the bewildering variations of the spectrum interlaced, blended, fell apart in showers of unbelievable hues, reformed, wavered, burst in skyrocket blooms of scarlet, vermilion, emerald, crocus, violet and gold that rushed together to form a veil of royal purple, burst anew to birth fresh miracles of mosaic tints.

It was the fire raging in the canyon, of course, the glow of the flames scrambled by the trillions of drops of falling water and transformed into an unearthly beauty that defied description. Slade felt it was worth all he had undergone to witness such a sight.

Gradually the phantasmagoria of color dimmed and faded to misty gray, purified to clear green once more. Evidently the fire had burned itself out and the fierce up-draft was freeing the canyon of smoke.

Slade waited a little longer although the damp cold was eating into his bones and he was numb and cramped from his strained position. Finally he concluded he could stand the discomfort no longer. He edged along his precarious perch and dived through the wall of falling water to the open air. The heat struck him like the breath of a blast furnace but was not unendurable. Finding a stone that was not quite redhot, he slumped wearily onto it and fumbled papers and tobacco from a waterproof pouch he carried for just such emergencies. A leisurely smoke helped a lot and he took stock of his surroundings.

The canyon was completely burned out. Of the luxuriant growth of chaparral there remained only charred trunks and occasional stout branches which resisted the onslaught of the flames. Spurtles of acrid smoke arose from still-sizzling patches of green and everything was covered with a thick coating of ash. The trail, however, was clear save for occasional falls of debris.

For an hour or so, Slade rested on the gradually cooling boulder. His strength revived, he set out down the canyon.

The gorge was still hot as an oven, but only a few feeble flickers remained of the conflagration. He found the bodies of the two horses, the roan and the outlaw's mount, burned to a crisp. Of the rigs nothing was left except the metal work. He was glad that he had been using a spare rig, lighter than Shadow's pet outfit, and more suited to the roan's lesser weight. With a sigh of relief he left the gorge of death and began the weary trudge back to the Slash S ranchhouse. His rifle, well greased, had suffered no harm from its wetting and he held it at constant readiness, although he did not expect that the outlaws had hung around for long after firing the canyon. He rather hoped they had, for he was in a mood for retaliation and would have enjoyed lining sights with the hellions.

The dawn was not far off when, weary to death, he reached the ranchhouse. A light burned in the living room and he found Ellen sitting up waiting for him. Her eyes were wide with apprehension as he stumbled into the room.

'Good heavens!' she exclaimed. 'What happened to you? You look half dead.'

'Feel sort of that way,' he admitted, slumping into a chair.

'And you've been in the water,' she said, 'Your clothes are all wrinkled and covered with soot. Never mind telling me now; wait till you've rested.'

'Okay,' he replied. 'And right now I'd like to voice your father's favorite question: May I have something to eat?'

'There's hot coffee on the stove and I've kept your dinner warm for you,' she told him. 'I'll put everything on the table as soon as you are ready to eat.'

He stood up, stretching his long arms over his head, his fingertips almost touching the ceiling.

'Feel better already,' he announced. 'I'll wash up a bit, in back at the hands' bench and I'll be all set. Stay away! You'll get all dirty.'

'To blazes with it!' she exclaimed as her arms went around him.

'And that helped a lot,' he chuckled, after a long moment. 'Even though your classic nose is all smudged.'

After he finished eating, Slade told her everything. 'At least I've learned how stolen cattle can be run from the valley without crossing the Hargus holding,' he concluded.

'But they'd have to cross the Mason land,' she remarked.

'Yes, they'd have to cross the Mason land,' he conceded, his voice hardening.

Ellen gazed at him a moment, her beautiful eyes speculative; but she asked no questions.

'Now to bed with you,' she said. 'You're half asleep already. Come on!'

Fourteen

When he awoke, around noon, Slade found himself a bit stiff and sore, with a few bruises to remind him of his tumble from the horse, but otherwise feeling quite fit and with no really bad results from his harrowing experience. Stewart was out on the range when he descended to the living room. Ellen sat with him while he ate his breakfast.

'I told Dad everything,' she said. 'He nearly blew up; I thought he'd have a stroke. And he's gone to packing a gun again, after years without one. He says he'd welcome a chance to shoot somebody; he means it.'

'Yes, I've a notion he does,' Slade chuckled. 'Well, it's a good notion for him to go heeled. Give him a much better chance to take care of himself if something should happen to break. But I'll say, and I'm not doing it just to comfort you, that after what happened yesterday, which was a failure, the danger to him has somewhat lessened.'

'What do you mean by that?' she asked.

'I mean,' Slade replied, choosing his words with care, 'that because of certain conclusions which I believe certain people have arrived at, that so long as I remain alive, nothing would be gained by the persons in question from doing away with your father.'

'That's nice, very nice,' she replied. 'Just wonderful! So now you are the target for those—I'd like to use the expressions Dad uses to describe, but I suppose I mustn't—persons who have been plotting to murder him. Yes, that makes me feel just wonderful!'

For a moment, Slade was moved to laugh at her white anger, but quickly decided not to, for she had spoken with blazing eyes and a rising voice and a clasping and opening of her slender fingers and was definitely in no mood for mirth.

'I think I am better able to take care of myself than your father is to take care of himself, because of which I am glad their attention has turned to me,' he said gently. 'Don't worry your pretty head; I have no intention of being killed if I can help it, and I think I can.'

'I hope so, and I have every faith in your ability,' she said moodily; 'but I can't help worrying. Dad is worried for you, too, and so will Andy Hargus be when he hears about what happened yesterday. He was here yesterday afternoon.'

'How did he and your father get along?' Slade asked curiously.

'Fine! They talked cattle and other things for quite a while. I believe that now when they've become acquainted and there are no differences between them that Dad has taken a liking to him.'

'And you?'

'Oh, I like him, too,' she answered. 'I think it would be hard for anybody who really knows him not to like him. He's just like a big woolly tame bear.'

Slade chuckled and regarded her with amused eyes. She smiled, a little wistfully.

'Cart Mason, who hasn't been here since the funeral, sent word he'd drop in this evening,' she added.

'And how do you like him?' Slade asked soberly. Ellen shrugged daintily.

'Oh, I suppose he's all right,' she replied. 'He's interesting and entertaining, and very good looking. But somehow I never cared much for his company. He looks at me. Oh, I don't mean that way; no woman minds a man looking at her that way, as you know darn well, even though it may cause her to shiver a bit sometimes. It's hard for me to put in words just how he looks at me. He—well, he looks at me as a man does at a piece of machinery that should prove useful, as if I were part of—a plan!'

'Or a plot,' Slade interpolated, his face

143

hardening.

'Yes, I suppose so,' she conceded. 'But how in the world could I be part of a plan, or a—plot?'

'I believe I heard you mention to Andy Hargus, the day Tom Hargus was buried, that your brother died when you were quite young,' Slade reminded her.

'That's right,' she admitted. 'He died when I was only ten.'

'Which leaves you in something of the nature of an only child.'

'I suppose so,' she replied, gazing at him in a puzzled fashion.

'And all your father's properties—very valuable properties—settle on you.'

'I suppose so,' she repeated. 'What in the world are you getting at, Walt?'

'And if your father had been killed and you found yourself alone in the world, Cart Mason might well have caught you on the rebound and persuaded you to marry him?' Slade pursued inexorably.

'Why—why, I suppose it would not have been beyond the realm of possibility,' she conceded.

'Well?'

She stared at him, and her eyes widened with horror. 'Walt,' she said, her voice little above a whisper, 'Walt you don't mean that Cart Mason—'

'Ellen,' he interrupted, 'I make no charges

144

that I can't prove, and I can prove nothing
against Cart Mason or anybody else, yet.'

'But you believe it,' she said. 'Well, tonight
will be the last time Cart Mason ever shows up
here, and he won't stay long this time.'

'Ellen, dear,' Slade said, 'will you do
something for me if I ask you?'

Her eyes met his. 'I think I've already
proven that I'll do anything you ask me to do,'
she replied.

'Yes, but this won't be pleasant.'

'Nevertheless I'll do it, if you ask me to,' she
repeated. 'What is it?'

'I want you to be nice to Cart Mason
tonight, even a little nicer than usual,' Slade
replied slowly. 'In other words, try to keep him
guessing a bit.'

'All right,' she said. 'It won't be easy, but I'll
do it if you ask me to. Oh, I'll get away with it.
Remember, my sex is the sex of subterfuge.'

'So a certain cynical philosopher once said,'
he replied smilingly. 'Personally, I think he
generalized a bit too much.'

'Don't be too sure,' she warned. 'You may
learn differently, to your cost.'

Slade laughed, and did not comment.

'Walt,' she said suddenly, 'supposing Dad
had been—killed, and I had married Cart
Mason?'

'I think,' Slade replied grimly, 'that you
might not have lived very long."

'You mean that—he would have murdered

me to get control of my inheritance?'

'If ordered to do so.'

'Ordered?'

'Yes, by a much smarter and even more ruthless man who, in my opinion, has some power over the Mason brothers, so that they are forced to do his bidding. I would say he is in possession of knowledge concering the Masons that they cannot afford under any circumstances to have revealed.'

Ellen shook her head. 'It's a wonder they don't kill him, if they are what they appear to be,' she remarked.

'Doubtless they would, only I imagine he is shrewd enough to have made provisions which will guarantee that in case of his death, the knowledge he has will immediately be made public. Not that the Masons need much urging to go along with him, I expect. There are men who will do anything for gain. And in this instance they are playing for big stakes; if all your father's holdings were totalled up, I don't doubt they would come close to half a million dollars, and that's a stake worth some little risk.'

The girl shuddered. 'It doesn't seem possible that such men exist!' she exclaimed.

'They do,' Slade said flatly. 'Fortunately, however, you don't often run across many with the ability to concoct such a fantastic scheme as this one. Which, were it not for an unforeseen incident, would very likely have

146

achieved a successful consummation.'

Again she raised her eyes to his. 'And you were the unforeseen incident,' she said.

'Possibly,' he conceded, 'but largely by accident. By way of what I would call a lucky break.'

'Sometimes,' she said wearily, 'I almost wish Dad was a cowhand working for wages; a lot of money can be a curse.'

'Not necessarily,' he differed. 'Your father could put his wealth to good use, as many men who have achieved financial success have done.'

'He is generous,' she said. 'He has helped many who never knew from where the help came. He does things that way.'

Slade nodded and did not look surprised.

'Remember,' he said, a note of warning in his voice, 'all that I've told you is in confidence and must go no further; it's strictly our secret.'

Her eyes, which had been somber, danced. 'That has a familiar ring,' she said. 'Don't worry, I don't intend to talk—about anything.'

The arrival of old Blaine ended the conversation. He shook hands warmly with Slade.

'So you came through it okay,' he said. 'The blankety-blank sons of skunks! I'm all set for 'em, too. See?'

He flipped his old Smith & Wesson from its sheath and turned it, the butt smacking accurately to his palm.

'Good speed,' Slade complimented him, as the gun slipped back into the holster.

'Think you could beat it?' the rancher asked. Slade smiled. 'Reach!' he said.

Stewart 'reached'—and looked into two black muzzles before his hand gripped the butt of the Smith.

'Heck and blazes!' he swore. 'I never saw anything like it! The "fastest gunhand in the whole Southwest," eh? I believe it.'

'I'm not so sure,' Slade said. 'I think I've seen men who could shade me if they tried.'

Stewart shook his head doubtfully. 'Wyatt Earp, perhaps?'

'Earp is fast, but not outstandingly fast,' Slade replied. 'On the other hand, he is deadly accurate; he never misses. The man who hopes to down him must do it with the first shot; he'll never get another. And during all his years as a peace officer, Wyatt Earp was never touched by lead. That record, I think, is unique. At least I never heard of it being equalled.'

'I doubt if you ever will,' nodded Stewart.

'And now if you little boys are through playing, I'll see that you get something to eat, Dad. We'll have coffee with him, Walt.'

'That's the best thing you've said yet,' her father agreed heartily.

After he had finished his meal, Stewart turned to Slade.

'I want to ride to town and see Hodson Vane,' he said. 'Do you mind riding with me?

Everything 'pears to be going smoothly on the range.'

'I'll be pleased to,' Slade said, and meant it. He also wished to see Hodson Vane, for a reason of his own.

Although he did not expect any trouble on the open range in broad daylight, Slade rode watchful and alert, not wishing to commit another blunder like the day before. Had he been paying more attention to what had been going on around him he wouldn't have found himself in such a hazardous position. He had no desire for a repetition or anything resembling it.

They reached Alforki without mishap. Stabling their horses, they made their way to the *Herald* Building. As usual, old Blaine walked into the editorial office unannounced. Hodson Vane looked up from his desk at their entrance, his jaw sagged slightly and for a moment his eyes mirrored something very like amazement, and perhaps a touch of fear. Slade saw that it was with an effort that he recovered his poise and greeted them casually. Slade nodded, and smiled thinly. Vane's eyes slid away from his.

'This is a surprise,' he said, and Slade felt sure he meant it.

'Yes, a surprise,' he repeated; 'I wasn't expecting you today, Mr. Stewart, but I have some proofs for you.'

Old Blaine, however, waved them aside. 'I

want to insert a reward notice,' he said, 'and run it every issue. I'm offering five thousand dollars reward to anyone who can provide information as to who is stealing my cows and molesting my hands. If that doesn't get results, I'll raise the ante to ten thousand.'

'Why—why certainly, Mr. Stewart,' Vane replied. 'I'll take care of it right away.'

'See that you do,' growled old Blaine. 'I'm fed up with the hell-raising hereabouts and I intend to get to the bottom of it or know the reason why. Come on, Walt, let's go get a drink.'

With another growl he left the office. From the corner of his eye, Slade saw Hodson Vane staring after them, a perplexed expression on his face. The ranger had difficulty suppressing a grin.

As soon as the outer door closed on their backs, Hodson Vace beckoned the man he had summoned to his office on the occasion of their first visit, some days before. Again he closed the door.

*   *   *

'What happened yesterday is a bit too much,' Stewart said as they headed for the Four Deuces. 'If something had happened to you, I'd never have forgiven myself.'

'It wouldn't have been your fault, sir,' Slade said gently.

'Like blazes it wouldn't!' snorted the rancher. 'I hired you, didn't I? And you were trying to find out what became of my stock, wasn't you? I hold that makes me responsible. If something had happened to you I'd have felt as bad about it as I would if it had happened to my own boy, who died when he'd just turned twenty. Come to think of it, you sort of remind me of him. He was tall, too, not as tall as you, but tall, and big. Had sort of the same kind of eyes that laugh one minute and look death and destruction the next. Funny, ain't it, how a big strong feller like him could be knocked over by a little bug you can't see with the naked eye. That's what killed him, the doctor said, a little bug called a pneumonia germ. Guess that was the way it was intended, though. I miss him. Had hoped he'd take over when I passed on. Yes, I miss him. My gal's fine, but she ain't a son. I miss him, and I get lonesome for him at times, especially in the evening when the sun sets and I get to thinking that my own time can't be far off and I wonder what's beyond the sunset. Yes, I get lonesome for him then.'

Slade's cold eyes were all kindness and his voice was very gentle when he spoke; for this confession bursting from the old man's lonely heart touched him deeply.

'He'll be waiting for you—beyond the sunset,' he said.

Old Blaine sighed. 'I hope so,' he said. 'I like to think he will be, and it's nice of you to

151

say so. He had a way of saying things like that, too, things that made me feel good. Maybe that's why I've took to you like I have, because you're—like him. Oh, the devil! Let's go get that drink.'

Truly, Slade thought, Blaine Stewart might well say with the prophet of old

For what hath man of all his labour, and of the vexation of his heart, wherein he hath laboured under the sun? For all his days are sorrows, and his travail grief; yea, his heart taketh not rest in the night.

Fifteen

The first person they saw when they entered the Four Deuces was Andy Hargus. He waved to them to join him at the bar.

'Heading back to the spread in a little while,' he announced as he motioned to the bartender. 'Came to town to order some supplies. How is everything?'

'Fine as frog hair,' said Stewart, who appeared to have thrown off his somber mood. 'I'll tell Ellen I saw you.'

'Thanks,' replied Hargus. 'Give her my best. Hope to get up your way soon.'

'We'll be glad to have you,' said Stewart. 'Anything new?'

152

'Nothing much, except Wes Mason got a bad shaking up. Horse fell with him, he said. Face all skinned, and he was limping. I saw him earlier in the day. He's gone home now.'

Old Blaine clucked sympathetically. Slade again had difficulty stifling a grin.

'There's Clyde Hartsook down at the other end of the bar,' Hargus remarked. 'Clyde sort of runs things over in the east valley,' he explained to Stewart.

'Call him over to have a drink with us,' old Blaine suggested. Hargus shot him a slightly surprised look. He moved down the bar and spoke to Hartsook, who accepted the invitation and joined them.

'Don't believe you've met Clyde, Mr. Stewart,' Andy said. The two men shook hands.

'How are things going with you?' Stewart asked.

'Not bad, despite the dryness,' Hartsook replied. 'I'm a bit short of water over there, otherwise nothing to complain about.'

Slade looked contemplative. 'Judging from the configuration of the hills and the slopes over there, I've a notion a few artesian wells might solve your problem,' he remarked.

'Really think so?' said Stewart. Slade nodded.

'But drilling wells, getting a rig here, and so on, costs money,' Hartsook said. 'I'm afraid I'm not in a position to swing it right now.'

'By gosh, that gives me an idea,' said Stewart. 'Fact is, I was planning to do a little drilling myself—' Which Slade knew was a prevarication of the first water. Again he bit back a grin.

'Yep, I was figuring on that,' Stewart repeated. 'The real cost is getting the rigs here. Once those work dodgers are here, they might as well earn their money. So I'll just send 'em over to your place and have them punch a few holes there while they're at it.'

'Why—why that's mighty nice of you, Mr. Stewart,' Hartsook said, and for the first time Slade saw his expressionless features register something akin to emotion.

'Take care of it first thing next week,' old Blaine said cheerfully. 'This is Friday; should have them on the job by Tuesday or Wednesday. Let's have another drink.'

After again expressing his gratitude, Hartsook moved back down the bar, where he had been holding a conversation. Andy Hargus sauntered along with him for a moment.

'The old man sure has changed a lot,' Hartsook commented. 'I can't understand what's come over him.'

'I can tell you,' Hargus replied; 'it's Slade. That big jigger's the limit. He can make a feller change his way of thinking by flip-flopping him through the air or by just looking at him. *He's* what I can't understand. And blast it! There are folks who swear he's an outlaw, an almighty smart one that nobody can pin anything on. Not that I give a hang one way or the other. Whatever he is, I'm for him.'

Hartsook laughed. 'Andy,' he said, 'have you ever been an outlaw?'

'Nope, I guess not,' Hargus admitted. 'I'm too scary to bust the law.'

'Well, as you know, I have been. We know our kind when we meet them.'

'And Slade?'

Hartsook's brittle voice became grim. 'Before all is finished, I'll guarantee there are people in this section who will wish the devil he was. And, incidentally, I predict that old Blaine Stewart is in for the surprise of his life. And it'll be good for him, and for a lot of other folks.'

'Now what the devil do you mean by that?' demanded Hargus.

Hartsook laughed again, and refused to comment further. Hargus gave up and rejoined Stewart and Slade.

'Mr. Stewart, that's a fine thing you're doing for Clyde,' he said. 'Those little creeks that give him water are just about empty because of the dry spell, and you can't grow cows proper without water.'

'If Slade knows what he's talking about, and I reckon he does, he'll get it,' Stewart replied. ' 'Pears to be a right sort of feller, kinda salty looking, but okay.'

'He is,' said Hargus. 'Made some mistakes

155

when he was young and sort of wild, but lived 'em down and is doing all right.'

'Guess we all make 'em,' grunted old Blaine. 'I sometimes think I got a positive genius for it. Well, all this palaverin' makes me hungry. Come on, Andy, and have a bite with us before you head for home.'

Hargus ate hurriedly and departed, for it was already quite late.

'Got a big day ahead of me tomorrow,' he explained. 'Plenty to do. Roundup time is going to be breathing down our necks 'fore we know it. Thanks for everything, be seeing you.'

Slade and Stewart dawdled over their meal, talking and watching the activities of the busy place. They lingered over coffee and cigarettes discussing various phases of ranch work, including the coming roundup.

'Got a notion it is going to be sort of different this year,' Stewart remarked. 'Last year it seemed everybody was on the prod against everybody else; we all had our bristles up. Roundup is hard work, but if it's handled right it can be lots of fun, too. Gathering around the fires at night, spinning yarns and singing and playing cards. Believe you said you played the guitar, didn't you? Well, I'll make it my business to get one. We oughta have some high old times this year.'

'No reason why we shouldn't,' Slade agreed.

It was getting along toward midnight when they left the Four Deuces, got the rigs on their broncs and headed for home. Old Blaine was in a jovial mood and hummed softly to himself as they rode along under the glitter of the stars.

Slade, on the other hand, was silent and thoughtful. Before they had covered half a mile from town, he abruptly veered Shadow's nose to the east.

'Hey! Where you going?' Stewart asked in surprise. 'The trail's over this way.'

'I know, but we're not using it,' Slade replied. 'We're taking a roundabout way home this time. Tonight I wouldn't ride through the gulley where we had the ruckus with the wideloopers for all your holdings.'

'What in blazes!' Stewart exclaimed, as he followed Slade away from the trail. 'Do you think somebody might be holed up there layin' for us?'

'In the light of what's been happening hereabouts of late, I don't consider it beyond the realm of possibility,' the ranger replied. 'We'd be sitting quail for anybody holed up in the brush alongside the trail; they'd down us before we knew what was happening. Might even be able to arrange things to make it look like we had a falling out and gunned each other. Such things have happened.'

Old Blaine swore sulphurously. 'Believe me, I'd love to line sights with the blankety-blank-blanks!' he concluded.

'If you don't mind taking a risk, you may get the chance,' Slade said.

'I'll take a risk,' Stewart growled. 'Just show me the chance.'

'If we should spot somebody holed up and waiting to mow us down, we would be within our rights in making a citizen's arrest of anybody perpetrating or contemplating a crime,' Slade explained. 'And if we managed to grab one of the devils, he might be induced to talk and perhaps help clean up this mess. I think it's worth taking a chance, if an opportunity should present.'

'I think so, too,' Stewart agreed. 'And I hope it does. I'm sick and tired of being hunted like a mad skunk. Let's go; you give the word and I'll trail with you.'

'We'll ride parallel to the trail but out of easy rifle shot till we reach that belt of thick brush which flanks the gulley, then we'll try and slide across to it and ride in its shadow,' Slade said. 'If they do intend to make a try for us, that's the logical place for a nice drygulching.' He glanced at the eastern sky. 'There'll be a moon a little later,' he added. 'It may be a hindrance or it may be a help, according to how things shape up.'

Riding straight across the prairie until Slade judged the distance sufficient, they turned north and continued at a fair pace. After a while the belt of brush loomed darkly on their left. Slade pulled up and studied it a moment.

'Quite a few thickets between here and the outer edge of the chaparral,' he commented. 'I

158

think we can risk it now; their attention, if they're in there, will be directed toward the trail. Or at least I hope so.'

Crossing the stretch of comparatively open territory was a ticklish business, even though they carefully kept the patches of thicket in line, and Slade felt decidedly relieved when they reached the darker shadow of the chaparral belt. He glanced anxiously at the eastern sky, saw it was already brightening; the moon wouldn't be long in arriving, and then they would be bathed in its silver light. That, however, was the chance they had to take.

'Hold it,' he suddenly exclaimed. They pulled to a halt and sat listening, Stewart shooting an inquiring glance at his companion but asking no questions.

The night was very still, with only the persistent hooting of an owl some little distance ahead to break the silence. Slade sat in an attitude of listening for another moment, then he said, 'Hear that owl? Listen to him whine. Something near his perch has him bothered.'

'A coyote, maybe,' Stewart guessed. Slade shook his head.

'A coyote wouldn't set him off that way or bring that querulous note to his call. If a coyote yipped, he'd answer, but not that way. And you'll notice there are no coyotes yipping hereabouts. When something disturbs a coyote, he keeps quiet. An owl talks.'

'Then what is it?' Stewart asked.

'I'd say there is a man or men holed up in the brush ahead,' Slade replied quietly.

'You mean the hellions we were talking about?'

'Quite likely. Don't see any legitimate reason for anybody to hide in the brush alongside the trail.'

'What we going to do about it?'

'See that thicket over to the right?' Slade replied. 'We'll tie the horses there and slip across to the chaparral on foot. Maybe we can worm our way in to where we'll get a sight of the devils. Have to be quiet, though. Very likely their nerves are on edge and they'll shoot at any unexpected sound. Think you can do it?'

'I can do it,' Stewart replied confidently. 'I know how to move in the brush. Did too much hunting in my younger days not to. Let's go!'

In the thicket they tethered Stewart's horse securely. Slade merely dropped the split reins to the ground, knowing that Shadow would not move when they were that way.

'Here comes the moon,' Slade said as they slipped from the thicket and made for the chaparral belt. 'Just in time to help, us, maybe.'

With the silver curve of the half moon just peeping above the horizon, they whisked across the open stretch and reached the chaparral without incident. Hugging the fringe of the growth, they proceeded cautiously

160

toward where the owl still complained.

As they edged along the ragged outer straggle, Slade cast apprehensive glances at the rising moon. Already objects that hitherto had been blurred and misty were clearly defined and developing clean-cut edges. And now there was almost no shadow to envelop them in its friendly gloom. If somebody was keeping tabs on the prairie! He had a highly uncomfortable feeling that even now a rifle barrel was lining in his direction, with evil, exultant eyes glinting along the sights. He might see the flash, but taking into account the speed with which a slug traveled, he would very likely not hear the report.

A moment later he called a halt; they were just about opposite where the owl in the brush close to the trail voiced its dislike for company that it did not understand and with which it did not desire a closer acquaintance.

'Now comes the ticklish part,' he breathed to Stewart. 'We've got to work through the brush without them hearing us till we spot them. Take it easy and keep right behind me. If they spot us first—'

He did not deem it necessary to complete the sentence. Old Blaine jerked his head in the affirmative and the nerve-tightening advance began.

From where they entered the growth to where it fringed the sunken trail was not much more than fifty yards, but it seemed a hundred miles and it took them full twenty minutes to negotiate it. The moon was well up, now, and pouring its pale radiance through rifts in the brush, washing the ground with ghostly patches of white light. These they detoured with the greatest care, careful to snap no twig, to tread on no dry and fallen branch. Almost overhead, the owl whined increased irritation. Was there no limit as to how many of those towering, mysterious and menacing things would keep materializing from the darkness? Thank Pete for wings!

Had Walt Slade been able to understand owl talk, he would have heartily concurred. At the moment, wings would have been a highly welcome adjunct.

For, although he was confident that the drygulchers might be within almost arm-length, he could see no signs of them. In a patch of deeper shadow, he and Stewart came to a standstill, afraid to move in any direction.

The owl was getting hoarse. The moon was climbing higher in the sky. But the gloom beneath the interlacing chaparral was deep save where the patches of moonlight silvered the ground. From sheer weariness of waiting, Slade was about to step boldly forward. And then the creeping moonlight revealed a slight movement near the lip of the brush-fringed trail. He tensed for instant action.

Two men stepped squarely into a patch of moonlight; each held a rifle in his hand.

Slade's voice rang out, shattering the stillness, causing the owl to give a dismayed whoop.

'Elevate!' he shouted. 'You recovered, and under arrest!'

For an instant the pair froze, motionless; then the rifles jutted forward. Slade fired twice, left and right; Stewart's gun boomed an echo as one of the rifles gushed flame. A slug whistled past. Slade fired again, and again.

One of the drygulchers whirled around and pitched headlong. The other dived into the brush and out of sight. Slade bounded after him, but before he reached the thorny tangle he heard a beat of fast hoofs fading into the distance.

'Careful,' he called to Stewart, who was approaching the body. 'If the hellion's only wounded he's as dangerous as a broken-back rattler.'

'This one won't ever be dangerous again,' the rancher replied. 'You got him dead center. Ornery looking specimen, ain't he?'

'Border scum, the sort that will murder anybody for a few pesos,' Slade said. 'Let's see what he's got on him.'

However, the dead man's pockets divulged nothing of significance. Slade returned the odds and ends and straightened up. Then he struck a match and held it close to the set countenance.

'Ever see him before?' he asked. Stewart

peered close.

'Darned if he don't look a mite familiar, but where I might have seen him I have no notion,' old Blaine replied. 'What shall we do with him—leave him for the sheriff?'

'We won't mention this affair to the sheriff or anybody else,' Slade decided. 'We'll just shove the carcass down the sag to the trail and leave it for somebody to find. If we say nothing it may puzzle the other devils, and somebody might say something or ask a question that would be of interest.'

'That's a notion,' agreed Stewart. 'Okay, down he goes.'

They hauled the body to the lip of the gulch and let it slide down to the bottom where it lay, dimly seen in the moonlight.

'I think I heard two horses moving away from here, but we'll have a look against the chance the bronc that hellion forked may be hanging around,' Slade said. 'Brand could possibly tell us something; unlikely, though.'

A careful search of the surrounding growth revealed nothing on four legs.

'Hightailed with the other one,' Slade remarked. 'Well, reckon we might as well head for home.'

Old Blaine nodded. His face looked strained and lined in the pale light.

'You did it again,' he said sententiously. 'If I'd been by myself or with some of the boys, I'd have sashayed right through that gulch.

Looks like you're sort of appointed to keep me alive.'

'Well,' Slade laughed, 'just so long as I succeed, there's nothing to bother our heads about. Let's go home.'

'My sentiments,' said Stewart. 'I'm hungry.'

*   *   *

Ellen was in the sitting room when they arrived. She gave Slade a significant glance and nodded. Old Blaine had something to eat and lumbered off to bed. Ellen left the room for a moment and then returned waving a lighted ribbon that disseminated perfume.

'What in blazes are you doing?' Slade wondered.

'Fumigating the house,' she replied. 'It is unnecessary, as I don't think he was infectious, but it relieves my feelings,'

She laughed and threw the remains of the ribbon into the fireplace.

'How did it go?' Slade asked. Ellen shrugged.

'I think I deserve to be congratulated for putting on a good act,' she answered. 'I was nice to him, perhaps a little too nice. For the first time he looked at me as if realizing I was a woman.'

'That,' Slade said, 'could lead to complications.' She shrugged again.

'I guess I can stand one more,' she said. 'I'm

165

getting used to it.'

Slade refrained from asking for an explanation. He felt called upon to acquaint her with the night's happenings. She listened wide-eyed and when he finished the account, she drew along and shuddering breath.

'I wonder how it's all going to end,' she said moodily. 'Appears to be getting worse all the time. You and Dad are in constant danger.'

'But we keep coming through all right,' he pointed out. 'So long as that obtains, there's nothing to worry about.'

'Yes, but how long can you expect your luck to hold? There's a limit, and the law of averages says it won't hold forever.'

'If your number isn't up, nobody can put it up,' he said.

'A very comforting fatalistic philosophy, but cannot one put one's number up by one's own acts? Such as by continually pushing into danger,' she retorted.

'There you have it,' he agreed. 'I hold that man is, to an extent, at least, the master of his own destiny, in this life and throughout the lives to come. He can rise to the heights or sink to the depths dormant in his nature. That is strictly up to him. And if he constantly seeks to rise, what happens to him in the process is really of infinitesimal importance.'

'That's better,' she conceded, 'but it still isn't pleasant to think of a threat constantly shadowing you.'

'Aren't we all constantly subjected to a threat of one sort or another? There is no escaping the inevitable; and Destiny is never thwarted.'

'It's hard to follow you, at times, but I think I understand,' she said. 'Oh, well!' She shrugged daintily and quoted, ' "Ah, fill the Cup—what boots it to repeat How time is slipping underneath our feet: Unborn Tomorrow, and dead Yesterday, Why fret about them if Today is sweet!" Today is all we have; we'll make the most of it!'

'Agreed!'

Sixteen

Slade was working in the office the following afternoon when Sheriff Dave Barnes rode up to the ranchhouse. The mumble of voices in the living room was followed by footsteps drawing nearer. Barnes and Stewart entered the office and closed the door. Behind the sheriff's back, old Blaine winked at Slade.

'The sheriff wants to talk to us,' he announced. 'Take a load off your feet, Dave, and loosen the latigo on your jaw.'

The sheriff sat down, and glowered at Slade. 'Well, what about it?' he demanded.

'What about what?' the ranger asked innocently.

'Blast it! You know what!' exploded the sheriff. 'About the feller who was picked up this morning on the Alforki Trail where it runs through that gully this side of town. Don't try to tell me you two didn't have something to do with it. I can't prove it, but I'll bet a hatful of pesos you did.'

Slade nodded to Stewart, who told him, in language unsainted. As the tale progressed, the sheriff's lined countenance looked very tired and old.

'Things are plumb out of control,' he said heavily when Stewart paused. 'Killings! Wideloopings! Attempted killings! I don't know which way to turn, and every way I do turn I'm up against a stone wall.'

'Don't let it worry you, Dave, it's a long worm that has no turning,' Stewart misquoted. 'You'll end up on top of the heap.'

'I wish I could believe it,' the sheriff replied pessimistically.

'Did anybody in town remember seeing him before?' Slade asked.

'Why, yes,' Barnes answered. 'He worked some as a swamper in the Four Deuces. Did odd jobs, like washing type and sweeping up over at the *Herald* Building. Hodson Vane remembered him. Said he was a good worker and tended to his own business and never bothered anybody. Vane seemed sort of shocked to hear about it.'

'Not surprising,' Slade commented. The

sheriff nodded.

'Always sort of hits you when a feller you know is picked up with a slug through him,' he said. 'But who in blazes would think that a jigger like that would be mixed up in such a business as last night. You don't know who to trust or to watch out for.' He shook his head at Slade.

'I don't put over much stock in the yarns some folks tell about you, but one thing is sure for certain; you're a bad luck piece if there ever was one. Whenever you squat in a section, trouble busts loose in every direction.'

'Sometimes when I leave it stops,' Slade answered smilingly.

'I don't doubt that one bit,' the sheriff concurred heartily. 'When do you figure to pull out?'

''Pears to me that he's stopped more trouble than he's started, right from the beginning,' Stewart observed. 'He's prevented killings, kept cows from being widelooped, brought folks together who weren't getting along.'

'I ain't arguing it,' sighed the sheriff. 'But I could sure stand a little peace and quiet for a change.'

'You'll get it,' Slade predicted, 'and you'll be plumb bored in consequence. See if I'm not right. Incidentally, it would please both Mr. Stewart and myself if you will regard what we told you as strictly confidential.'

'All right,' grunted Barnes. 'I'll keep my trap shut. Don't know why you want me to, but I will.'

The sheriff had coffee and a snack and then headed back to town in a somewhat better temper.

'Poor old Dave,' observed Stewart. 'He's all worked up. Can't blame him, though; things have been sort of jumping of late and 'pear to be getting no better fast. What I'd like to know is who in the devil is back of all this trouble.'

'I predict you'll be sort of surprised when you learn,' Slade replied grimly.

'I don't doubt it,' growled Stewart. 'Getting so I'm looking sideways at most everybody. I don't trust myself when I'm shaving. Do you realize that hellion was on my own payroll! I think I'll go out to the kitchen and see if Charley's got a bottle of arsenic hid away somewhere.'

'Charley's methods would be direct,' Slade smiled. 'I think a meat-axe would be more in his line.'

Old Blaine chuckled. 'Guess you're about right,' he replied. 'Get him riled and he's a holy terror.'

'Mr. Stewart,' Slade suddenly asked, 'did the Mason brothers bring their riders with them when they moved to the Valley?'

Stewart shook his head. 'Nope,' he answered. 'They hired here. Got a nice bunch of fellers, most of 'em young. Some of 'em

170

born and raised right here in the Valley. The Harguses brought their hands with them. Sort of salty, but okay. Never heard anybody complain about them.'

Slade nodded thoughtfully, and changed the subject.

*   *   *

That night there was a meeting in the Mason ranchhouse that would have interested Walt Slade greatly. Behind a locked door and closed shutters, six hard-looking characters lounged about the living room talking and smoking. Behind another door, also locked, the Mason brothers, Cart and Wes, sat at a table with Hodson Vane, the editor of the Herald. Vane was talking.

'Well, it was muddled again,' he said, his tone indicating that there was no doubt in his mind as to who 'muddled' it.

Wes Mason flushed and his eyes were resentful. 'Yes, again. How, I don't know,' he conceded. 'Peyton, who managed to get away, said all he knows was that all of a sudden the big hellion was behind him and Carroway yelling they were under arrest. What I'd like to know is how in blazes did he get out of that canyon! It was a mass of fire from one end to the other, and he walked out unscorched.'

'They say the Devil lives in fire,' Carter Mason observed sententiously; 'I'm inclined to

171

believe there may be something to that yarn.'

'And I'm about ready to agree with you,' said Wes. Hodson Vane snorted his disgust.

'He's not the Devil,' he said, 'and it was nothing but your own confounded carelessness that let him get away. You should have stuck around and made sure he didn't escape the fire. You can't take any chances with his kind; he's fuller of tricks than the monkey house at the zoo. Yes, you should have stuck around. Why didn't you think of that?'

'If you'd just had your neck close to busted, maybe you wouldn't have thought of everything, either,' snapped Wes, tentatively caressing his still bruised face. 'Blast it! There seems no way to get the best of that hellion.'

'He's not the Devil,' Vane repeated, 'and he's not invulnerable. It's your own fumbling and stumbling that's to blame. You couldn't even do for Tom Hargus without bungling it. If you keep on the way you're going, you'll be lucky not to stretch rope for that one. The devil only knows what Slade was able to make of that; I suppose you left a handful of clues lying around for him to pick up.'

Wes Mason's face whitened with anger. His right hand raised slightly from the table on which it rested. Vane eyed him steadily, the fingers of his left hand lightly caressing the left lapel of his coat.

'Don't try it, Wes,' he advised in pleasantly conversational tones. 'Chances are I'd kill you before you could slide that sleeve gun into your hand, and even if you managed to shade me, which I doubt, you'd slip the noose over your own head by doing so. Don't forget, everything needed to hang both of you is carefully placed so that it would be made public if I should happen to pass on suddenly. *Don't—forget!'*

Wes Mason's eyes still flamed, but he dropped his hand. Cart, who had gone rigid, relaxed.

'Don't be a fool, Wes,' he said, 'and, Vane, nothing is gained by this bickering. We've got to stick together or we'll all hang, or eat lead. Wes and me are doing the best we can, and that's all there is to it. What you're both doing is forgetting to give Slade credit. He didn't tie onto the name *El Halcon* for nothing. He's just what that name means, as swift and deadly as a hawk. And he thinks as fast as he reaches for a gun. What we've got to do is outsmart him, not go getting our bristles up at each other when he outsmarts us. What happened last night was a fair example of his way of thinking. He knows we are out to get him and reacts accordingly. Stop and consider calmly a moment and you can think as he thought, that where the trail runs through the gulley was just where anybody with a drygulching in mind would likely try to stage it. So he slid around the gulley and somehow nosed out Peyton and Carroway and got the drop on them. It's a plumb wonder that Peyton managed to get away alive. I wish I knew for sure that Carroway didn't do any talking before he took the Big Jump. But Peyton was sure he was drilled dead center. I hope so. I repeat, Wes and I are doing the best we can, and you're supposed to be the brains of this outfit; you figured out the scheme in the first place. So try and figure some way to get us off the hot spot we're on right now. Looks like to me you aren't doing any too well, either.'

'I'll admit the truth of the allegation,' Vane said. 'But it's partly because of the tools I have to work with. You aren't even doing very well with the girl, and she's your private chore.'

'Don't be too sure,' Cart Mason replied. 'She was mighty nice to me last night. I think she's gotten over her infatuation for that big hellion, if she ever had one. I give her credit for brains enough to realize he's the here-today-and-gone-tomorrow sort. I think that angle will be taken care of, if Slade and old Blaine are taken care of. They're our big problem right now.'

'I don't know what the devil has come over Stewart,' Vane said. 'He seems to have lost interest in everything he used to turn his wolf on. I tried to show him the proofs of next week's article blasting the rangers and he wouldn't even take the trouble to look at them. He's gotten together with the Harguses and the people over in the east valley and I'm of

174

the opinion he does exactly what Slade tells him to do.'

'Well, you know *El Halcon*'s reputation,' said Carter Mason; 'homing in on things other people have started and skimming off the cream. What I'd like to know is how much does he know or has he guessed.'

'I don't see any reason for him to really know anything for sure,' countered Vane. 'Right now, with the Harguses eliminated as suspects, everybody figures an outfit from south of the Rio Grande is working the Valley, just as similar outfits have worked it before. Why should Slade think differently?'

'Because he's *El Halcon*,' growled Wes. Vane grunted disgustedly.

'The *El Halcon* myth has got you buffaloed,' he said. 'I think it's highly exaggerated.'

'Maybe,' conceded Wes, 'but if you'd seen him looking at you over gun sights as Cart and me did, you might think a mite different. I was looking straight at him and I never saw him reach. Those irons just "happened" in his hands.'

'Why didn't you use your famous sleeve draw on him after you had your hands up?' Vane asked sarcastically. 'That's how you killed the—'

'Stop it!' barked Wes. 'I did think of doing just that, but something seemed to tell me that if I tried it I'd be dead one second later. So I didn't try it. Right then we didn't know who he was—figured he was just a chuckline-riding cowpoke—and of course, we didn't want Tom Hargus' killing tied onto anybody other than one of the Stewart outfit. So after we had a minute to think, we went along with him and just pretended to know nothing. Then we proceeded to fill him up with reasons why the Stewart outfit might have done for Tom, without really saying so. Figured he swallowed it, then. I ain't so sure now.'

'All right,' said Vane. 'What's done is done and there's no use bothering our heads about it. As Cart said, we won't gain anything by snapping at each other and accusing each other of making mistakes. From now on, *Senor* Slade is my personal chore.'

'You're welcome to it,' Wes said heartily. 'Here's wishing you luck—you'll need it.'

'I'll make my own luck,' Vane replied. 'Call the boys in. You sure all your hands left for town? We don't want them snooping around and wondering what's going on.'

'I handed them a few extra pesos for doing good work getting ready for the roundup,' Carter answered. 'Told 'em to go to town and celebrate. They didn't need any urging.'

'Okay,' Vane nodded. 'Call the boys in.'

Carter Mason unlocked the door, opened it and beckoned to the occupants of the outer room. They filed in, looking expectant. Mason closed the door and locked it again.

176

Seventeen

Two days later another meeting, of a different sort, was held at the big Slash S ranchhouse. Every spread owner of Alforki Valley was present, each accompanied by his range boss. The object of the meeting was to make arrangements for the coming roundup, the fall or beef roundup for the purpose of gathering all cattle for shipment to market and for the branding of late calves or those overlooked in the spring or calf roundup when the winter's crop of calves was branded.

The fall roundup was conducted along much the same lines as that of the earlier part of the year, but the work was usually done with more deliberation, for the cows were heavier in flesh and fat, and it was important not to run more fat off them than necessary. Loss of weight meant loss of revenue at marketing time.

After some discussion it was determined that the south-central pasture of the Slash S would be the best and most convenient-to-all location for the holding spot where the herd would be worked, the various brands being cut out and segregated and made ready for shipping.

Next came the highly important matter of choosing a roundup boss whose word would be law, no matter if he did not own a hoof. The owners of the cattle would be as much under his orders as any common cowhand or wrangler.

Clyde Hartsook, owner of the C Lazy H spread, stood up. 'Gents,' he said, 'it's my opinion that we've got a man here who, though sort of new to the section, has more savvy and know-how of the cow business than any of us. I figure the Slash S range boss, Walt Slade, is the man for the chore.' There was a general nodding of heads.

'Brother Hartsook, we set store by your judgment,' remarked a lank old Kentuckian, 'and if you say Slade is the man for the job, I reckon there won't be many dissenting votes.'

There were no dissenting votes and Slade was unanimously elected to superintend the roundup. He stood up, towering over the men around him.

'Gentlemen, I thank you for your confidence,' he said. 'I'll try to make sure it isn't misplaced.'

'Reckon it won't be misplaced much,' chuckled Blaine Stewart. 'You've already done more for this section in a few weeks than anybody else has done in that many years.'

Again there was a general nodding of heads, and men pressed forward to shake hands with the new roundup boss and pledge all the assistance in their power.

'And now, gents, to the dining room and a surrounding,' said old Blaine. 'Ellen, break out a few of my private bottles. I figure this calls for a mite of celebrating, the first real roundup in Alforki Valley for a mighty long time. A week from tomorrow we'll start combin' the brush for those perambulatin' beefsteaks.'

True to his promise, Blaine Stewart had two drilling rigs at work on Clyde Hartsook's holding by the middle of the week. At his suggestion, Slade rode with him to the C Lazy H and, after a careful study of the terrain, chose the spots for the drilling, which caused the owner of the rigs to view him with some curiosity.

'Looks like you know considerable about this business, cowboy,' he observed. 'Usually takes an engineer to make those calculations.'

'Sometimes,' Slade replied with a smile. 'Guess I've just sort of got a knack for it.'

'Yes, quite a knack,' the drill man remarked dryly.

Old Blaine gazed complacently at the bits chugging into the soil. 'This ought to help a lot,' he said. 'And after they finish here, I think we'll scout around a mite and see if there ain't some other places that can stand a little attention. Good notion?'

'Very good,' Slade replied. 'These are your people, sir, your responsibility. You have been greatly blessed in this world's goods and its fine of you to extend a helping hand to those who have not received in such abundance.'

'Sort of intimating that I'm my brother's

keeper, eh?' chuckled Stewart.

'Well,' Slade smiled, 'according to the Scriptures, a gent once asked the Lord that question. As I recall, he got a mighty straight answer.'

'Yes, I guess that's so,' old Blaine agreed, nodding—soberly.

*   *   *

That night, Ellen spoke in a similar vein. 'It's truly amazing, the change in Dad,' she said. 'He takes little interest in the things that formerly obsessed him, and he is so much happier and content, so different from what he used to be.'

'Perhaps,' Slade replied gently, 'perhaps he has learned the joy that comes from service; he's busy all day doing good. That is apt to change one.'

She was silent for some moments, her eyes studying his face. Then, 'Walt, do you always affect people that way?'

'What way?' he countered with a smile.

'The way you have affected Dad. I can't altogether understand it, but there is something about you that compels one to do your will, as I have good reason to know.'

Slade's eyes danced. 'Perhaps I just point out to them what they've really been wanting to do all the time,' he replied.

'Perhaps in my case,' she retorted, blushing

180

a little and laughing a little. 'But not in Dad's, of that I'm positive. He was all wrapped up in the things that interested him, with little thought for anything or anybody else. He was convinced that what he was doing was the right thing to do.'

'Well, I don't think he's changed much, then,' Slade replied. 'He's thoroughly convinced that what he is doing now is the right thing to do.'

'Yes, but forwarding one's interests and desires is somewhat different from giving one's all in selfless service.'

The laughter left Slade's eyes when he replied, 'Perhaps you'll recall my saying the other night that of his own will, a man can sink to the depths or rise to the heights dormant in his nature. Well, I'd say that right now your father is very much on the upgrade, and that nothing is going to stop him.'

'I think you're right,' she said. 'In fact, I'm sure you're right; and it has made me very happy.'

'Then it was worth all the effort,' he replied. 'I want you to be happy.'

'I believe you,' she said, 'and I believe you would do all in your power to make me happy. But there are some things that it is not in your power to do.'

'Yes?'

'Yes. It is not in your power to change your nature, and an eagle can't be happy confined in a barnyard.'

'I think the aptness of the metaphor depends on one's conception of a barnyard,' he smiled. 'Perhaps our definitions differ.'

'Oh, you know what I mean,' she countered. 'Well, a dream is sometimes nice to remember, even after one awakens. You see I'm leading up to telling you something.'

'What's that?'

'Today,' she said slowly, 'Andy Hargus asked me to marry him.'

Slade did not show surprise. 'And your answer?'

'I told him I'd give it tomorrow,' she replied. 'What do you think it should be?'

'I think, considering your well being and happiness, that it should be "yes",' he said.

'I believe you're right,' she said. 'After all, I've no desire to end up an old maid trying to live on memories. So I think I'll tell Andy I will.'

'And I don't think you'll ever regret it,' he predicted. 'Then tomorrow I guess it's goodbye,' she said softly. 'I guess it'll have to be—tomorrow,' he agreed.

She laughed gaily. 'I'm glad you said it that way,' she whispered. 'Yes, it will be goodbye—tomorrow!'

Eighteen

Roundup days! Dust, and sun, and sweat! The whiff of wood smoke! The aroma, more fragrant to hungry men than all the spices of Arabia, of steaming coffee and frying bacon! The acrid stench of scorched hair and seared flesh! And sometimes the raw and piercing smell of fresh blood!

Days of toil, discomfort and danger; but evenings of jollity and good comradeship around the campfires. Then dreamless sleep beneath the glittering stars.

The cowboy learned to love and study the stars. They were his guide, his clock and his almanac. His friends, his solace in time of trouble, or grief, his understanding companions when he rode lonely night guard or the unreeling ribbon of the chuckline trail. They gazed a benediction when his eyelids closed, built up in him strength and courage to meet the new day with gladness and unafraid.

The roundup, an institution of the West, began as a getting together of a few neighboring stockmen to look over each other's herds for stray animals. These neighborhood gatherings were called cow hunts or cow work. From them grew the great wholesale operations in handling range cattle in the days of vast acreages, free grass and no fences. Not until barbed wire arrived did the roundup in the real sense of the word become practically extinct.

Cows don't recognize boundaries that are not plainly marked by unbreakable fence. Where the grass leads the cow goes and in the old days the stock of various holdings became intermingled. Thence the necessity of gathering together all the animals of a section and carefully cutting out and separating each owner's beefs. Calves were branded in accordance with the burn borne by the cow they followed. This was to an extent a hit-or-miss method but as a rule fairly reliable, although it did open the corral gate for some weird shenanigans on the part of persons of easy conscience. For instance, the fact that one enterprising gentleman's cows were having seven or eight calves a year might be passed over as a freak of unpredictable Nature; but when his bulls also began having calves, that was deemed a bit too much. So he was given a job making hair bridles for the state, under strict supervision.

All of which made the roundup if not a thing of beauty and a joy forever, at least something of interest, and the cowboy loved it.

Slade's first chore as roundup boss was to select from among the assembled cowboys certain assistants he believed to be of good judgment and experience. These would be in command of groups of hands that were to comb the range thoroughly in search of vagrant cows as well as large bunches. Giving special attention to thickets, coulees and canyons where old mossyhorns would hole up to escape the heat and interference with their activities.

Eager to begin their work, the groups hightailed away from the holding spot. Soon they would start to scatter, first dividing into small parties, which in turn broke up until each man had a section of ground over which to ride. He was responsible for all the cattle the section might contain. Where the ground was broken or brush-covered, careful searching was necessary to round up all the cows that might be hidden there. As soon as a hand had collected as many critters as he could manage he drove them to the holding spot. The captured cattle were surrounded and held in close herd until the cutting out and the branding commenced.

At noontime, when the hands trooped in to eat their midday meal, Slade inspected the herd and decided it was large enough to start separating and tallying the brands and driving them to each owner's individual holding spot.

'Okay,' he told a number of the punchers, 'fork your cutting cayuses and let's start unscrambling them.'

Soon the concentrated mass of cattle was invaded by cowboys mounted on horses that were, both by instinct and training, especially adapted to the difficult and dangerous work of cutting individual animals from the body of the herd.

Cutting called for daring and skillful horsemanship and Slade had chosen the men for the chore with care. In between the animal to be segregated and the bulk of the herd darted the trained bronc and after much dodging and ducking, accompanied by picturesque profanity on the part of the rider, the recalcitrant beast was shoved past the tally man and to its proper cut.

'Cutting is fascinating to watch,' Ellen Stewart, who had ridden from the ranch to the holding spot, remarked. 'But just the same it always frightens me a bit—no telling what might happen.'

'The boys know their business and aren't likely to make mistakes,' Slade reassured her. 'Watch this one, now; that's a real tophand shoving that cow.'

For a time everything went smoothly, and then it happened, the most dreaded accident of the range. A young hand from Clyde Hartsook's spread was after a huge old mossyhom whose rolling eyes and flaring nostrils bespoke an unusually vicious temper. The steer dodged, veered, slanted sideways. The cowboy, saying things he never learned in Sunday School, raced to cut it off. His horse swerved, stumbled and fell, hurling the rider through the air like a stone from a catapult to strike the ground with stunning force. The steer, with a bellow of rage, charged the prostrate and helpless puncher, needle-pointed horns lowered.

But before those lances of death could reach the cowboy, who was striving vainly to rise, a great black horse was alongside the charging steer. Walt Slade left the saddle in a streaking dive. His outstretched hands gripped the widespread horns at the base. A mighty wrench, his long body hurtling sideways, and over went the steer with a crash that knocked all the fight out of it. Instantly the hands were swarming over the bawling beast that Slade held helpless. In a trice it was roped. Slade got to his feet, dusting himself off.

The young cowboy had also risen to stand weaving a little. He stared at Slade.

'Feller,' he said, his voice a trifle unsteady, 'feller, I just looked across into eternity—and it wasn't far! Much obliged!'

'All in the day's work,' Slade laughed and sauntered to where Shadow stood patiently waiting, looking bored with the whole procedure.

Ellen was beside him, her face paper-white. 'You might have been killed!' she gasped.

Slade laughed again. 'Looks spectacular but really there's very little danger,' he replied. 'It was the steer that took the risk of having his neck busted.'

'I was lining sights with the hellion when

187

you grabbed him,' said old Blaine.

'No sense in making coyote bait of fifteen hundred pounds of beef,' Slade answered cheerfully; 'better to just shake him up a bit.'

'Uh-huh, but don't do it again,' Stewart ordered. 'There's a lot more risk to that sort of bulldoggin' than you let on there is. Plug the so-and-so!'

Day after day the work went on, with no further untoward incidents. Slade insisted that no spot where elusive critters might seek hiding be overlooked.

'I don't want any strays mavericking around after this cow gathering is over,' he said. 'Strays mean careless combing, and whoever is responsible for them will answer to me personally.'

With which in mind, the cowboys decided there would be no strays. And there weren't.

Finally all was done and the cows ready to roll to Marfa and the shipping pens. The great Slash S herd would lead the way.

'Biggest and finest bunch I ever shoved,' old Blaine said complacently, looking over the sea of shaggy backs and tossing horns. 'Best gol-darned roundup I ever had to do with. Walt, you're a wonder!'

The other owners voiced emphatic agreement. And Slade was unanimously elected trail boss of the drive.

So began the most picturesque and interesting feature of the cattle business, the movements of the herds going 'up the trail' to market.

The cows were not really driven—they were 'trailed', grazing their way in the right direction in a great arrowhead formation, point to the front.

That is, after the first day. The first day out, Slade pushed the herds so that when night came the cattle would be tired out and less liable to stampede or seek to stray back to their accustomed feeding grounds. After that they were allowed to take it easy, so as not to run the fat off them.

Although he did not really expect any trouble, Slade took no chances, for this was a wild country and cow thieves were experts at making sudden and unexpected raids, cutting out a number of valuable head and sliding them into some unknown canyon or gorge where it would be difficult and dangerous to pursue them. He posted double night guards and wherever possible had outriders scouring the country on either side of the marching column.

No one rode immediately in front of the herd. To do so would make the cows nervous and balky, for they didn't trust a man's back any more than they did his front and looked upon a horseman as a natural enemy and productive of trouble.

Near the head of the marching column rode the point men whose duty it was to veer the cattle when a change of direction was desired. One would ride in toward the leaders, the other drift away from them in the change of direction. The cows would shy away from the approaching rider and toward the one who was drawing away from them.

About a third of the way back behind the point men came the swing riders, where the herd began to bend when changing course. Another third of the way back were the flank riders. The duty of both swing and flank riders was to prevent sideways wandering and to drive off any foreign cattle that might seek to join the herd.

Bringing up the rear, cursing the heat and the dust and the slow or obstinate critters, were the drag riders, 'shovin' 'em along.' Then came the remuda of spare horses with a wrangler in charge. Last, the chuck wagon driven by old Charley Simpson to the accompaniment of appalling but jovial profanity.

The Hargus herd, in similar formation, followed about a quarter of a mile behind the Slash S, with the other outfits trailing along, one by one, the Mason brothers' Bar M bringing up the rear.

Usually the trail boss rode far ahead to survey the ground and locate watering places and good grazing ground for the night bedding down. In this instance, however, that was not necessary, there being men along who were familiar with the route and knew where the night halts should be made.

Traveling by easy stages, Slade figured to make Marfa by noon or a little later of the fourth day. Blaine Stewart concurred.

'No sense in pushing 'em,' he said. 'We're in no hurry and the prime notion is to get 'em there in first-class shape.'

The third night out, Slade sat with his back to a tree at the edge of a thicket and a little way off from the camp-fires, smoking and thinking. His reactions to the events of the past weeks were decidedly mixed. It would appear that he was quite a successful roundup and trail boss, and that he had undoubtedly gained considerable influence over old Blaine Stewart and he believed that, aided and abetted by Stewart's charming daughter, there was a chance of swinging the stubborn old rancher into line with his way of thinking. That was problematical, of course, but he was beginning to believe that it could be done.

But robbery and murder had been committed in the section. The perpetrators of the crimes must be brought to justice. And so far he felt he was getting exactly nowhere with the real mastermind who was back of the whole nefarious business. Well, maybe he'd get a break, but he had an uneasy premonition that the 'break' might be attended by circumstances far from pleasant.

Clyde Hartsook strolled over and with a nod

squatted beside the ranger and began the manufacture of a cigarette. Slade continued to smoke in silence. Hartsook took his time completing the brain tablet, eyed his handiwork with complacency and struck a match. He inhaled deeply, let the smoke trickle from his nostrils and spoke, 'About ready to make your throw?'

Slade shook his head. 'Not yet,' he replied. 'No proof, especially against the hellion I'm most anxious to drop a loop on. Suspecting is not proving, you know.'

'Reckon you a little more than just suspect, don't you?' queried Hartsook.

'Yes,' Slade answered. 'In my own mind I'm confident as to who is responsible for what's been going on, but that's not enough. I rather think I could get a conviction for Tom Hargus' murder against the other two, but the devil I really want might well wriggle out of the noose. He's cunning and resourceful and very likely covers his tracks as he goes, and in a manner hard to combat.'

'You'll get him, only a matter of time,' Hartsook predicted cheerfully.

'I hope so,' Slade replied. 'At least I've managed to scramble his neat little scheme for him. It was a beaut; tell you about it later.'

Hartsook shot him a shrewd glance and chuckled. 'I've a notion that arguing Miss Stewart into agreeing to marry Andy Hargus was a sort of master stroke,' he said.

Slade smiled. 'And the very best thing for both of them,' he replied.

'Right you are,' agreed Hartsook. 'That's what Andy needs, a smart woman who'll hold him in line, and he'll be good to her. I'm plumb pleased with the way that one worked out. And I'm sure you're going to come out on top before the last brand's run.'

'You've given me a lot of help, Clyde, and I won't forget it,' Slade said. 'You tied up some loose threads that were banging around and gave me my first real lead on the sidewinder.'

Hartsook nodded. 'As I said before,' he remarked, 'I can put up with a maraudin' grizzly, but I've no use for skunks.'

'I fear you malign the skunk,' Slade protested with a smile. 'He 'tends to his own business and never bothers anybody who doesn't bother him.'

'Uh-huh, but he smells out loud, and so does that other hellion,' grunted Hartsook.

Engrossed in their conversation, neither noted the furtive figure lurking just inside the thicket and within earshot.

Nineteen

In the dark hour before the dawn, Carter Mason, after a consultation with his brother, stole softly from the encampment, leading his saddled horse. When sure he was beyond hearing distance, he mounted and rode at top speed for Alforki. Arriving at the cattle town, he hitched his horse before the *Herald* Building. Behind a closed and locked door he recounted to Hodson Vane the conversation between Slade and Clyde Hartsook.

'The horned toad is some sort of an infernal law man, perhaps a Cattlemen's Association rider,' he concluded.

'More likely a Texas Ranger,' Vane said quietly.

'A ranger!' Mason exclaimed, his eyes wide. 'You going to put a bug in old Stewart's ear?'

'Would be just a waste of time,' Vane replied. 'Slade has him completely dominated. If I proved to him that the big hellion is the Devil himself, he'd still do exactly what Slade told him.'

'Then what in blazes are we going to do?' Mason demanded.

'We're going to pull out,' Vane said definitely. 'There's nothing else for us to do. Everything has gone completely haywire. The girl marrying Andy Hargus knocks our plan into a cocked hat. Yes, we've got to pull out, but I believe I can work it so we'll make a big haul first.'

'And I want that girl,' growled Mason. 'All of a sudden I've took a fancy to her.'

'You're loco!' protested Vane. 'Mixing a woman into such an affair is looking for trouble. You leave her alone.'

'Listen, Vane,' retorted Mason, 'you had the goods on Wes and me. You had the goods, but you haven't any more. We can only hang once, and somehow Slade's got the lowdown on us over the Tom Hargus killing. And maybe he knows about Joe Callison, too. And if we hang, you'll hang with us. The boot's on the other foot now, Vane, and you're going to string along with me. I say I want that girl, and I'm going to have her.'

'All right,' conceded Vane, his eyes glittering. 'We're in no position to be quarreling among ourselves over trifles. But I predict you'll be sorry. Laying a hand on a woman in this section is worse than a killing.'

'We won't be in this section,' Mason replied. 'Now what have you got in mind?'

'As soon as you get something to eat and a little rest, head for Marfa,' Vane said. 'The chances are you haven't been missed and you can slide into the town tonight without attracting any attention. When you get there, keep tabs on old Stewart. I figure he'll spend the night in Marfa—and head back to Alforki tomorrow morning. He won't make it here until after dark. Don't let him out of your sight, and when you get here, have Wes watch him and you come to me pronto. I think I can figure a way for us to make a good last haul and give *Senor* Slade his comeuppance at the same time. Do you understand?'

195

'Guess I do,' replied Mason. 'Okay, I got the powders and I'll follow your lead.'

*   *   *

Shortly after noon, the trail herds boomed into Marfa, a treeless, jackal-fringed settlement, the shipping point and supply depot for the ranches in the mountains to the north and south. The buyers were waiting, cash in hand, and rejoiced at the fine shipments brought them. With smooth efficiency and dispatch the weighing-in and the loading from the pens up the chutes and into the strings of waiting stockcars were accomplished. Before nightfall the last long train crammed with its bawling charges rumbled east. Slade and old Blaine watched the last set of red rear markers bob out of sight.

'Well, that's that, and it paid off,' the rancher remarked complacently. He tapped the bulging wallet tucked in his inside coat pocket. 'A hefty passel of dinero there,' he added. 'Better'n thirty thousand pesos. Yep, I'm loaded.'

'And you want to stay that way,' Slade said. 'No prowling around by yourself tonight, packing all that money.'

'Garner and Fulton will be riding herd on me every minute,' Stewart replied.

Slade nodded. Garner and Fulton were two salty oldtimers who had been with Stewart for years. Had they been the sort to carve notches, the gun barrel of each would have accommodated quite a few.

'Not that I figure there's much danger of anything happening here,' Slade observed. 'Just the same we'll take no chances, and when you get back to Alforki you really want to watch your step.'

'You're darn right,' grunted Stewart. 'Too blasted many off-color happenings thereabouts of late.'

Feeling a desire to be by himself for a while, Slade explored the town, which was not particularly interesting, although the presence of the trail crews had it bustling at the moment. He was having a bite to eat in a restaurant-saloon some time later when Clyde Hartsook strolled through the swinging doors and dropped into the opposite chair.

'Somehow I got a notion something's in the wind,' the C Lazy H owner remarked without preamble. 'Cart Mason wasn't with his herd at the weighing-in or the loading. Then all of a sudden, after dark, he showed up and he and Wes are together in a bar up the street. He'd been somewhere and just got back. What do you make of it?'

'Hard to tell,' Slade replied. 'Very likely we'll find out, and it will be something unpleasant.'

'Well,' Hartsook said, rising, 'I'm going to keep an eye on that pair from now on. They're up to no good, I'll bet a hatful of pesos.'

"That'll be a help, Clyde, and thank you for your interest,' Slade replied.

'Got a soft of personal axe to grind for that pair,' Hartsook said, with a grin. 'Oh, nothing they've done to me. I just don't like 'em.'

With a wave of his hand he strode out. Slade returned to his dinner.

The night passed uneventfully and early the next morning the Alforki Valley outfits headed for home. The chuck wagons and the remudas would follow at a more leisurely pace.

It was well past dark when they reached town and everybody was starved.

'No getting to the bank today,' Stewart observed as he and Slade headed for the Four Deuces and something to eat. 'Oh, well, it doesn't matter. Take care of it tomorrow.'

After they had finished eating and had a drink and a smoke, Slade said, 'I think I'll drop over and see Sheriff Barnes; haven't had a palaver with him for quite a while. Here come Garner and Fulton to ride herd on you.'

'I'm okay with that pair hanging around,' Stewart chuckled. 'Go ahead, don't bother about me.'

Slade found the sheriff in an expansive mood. 'Looks like things might quiet down for a spell,' he said. 'I just got back from the county seat. Sort of a stranger there of late. All quiet there, though, and I got a good chief deputy to look after routine matters. How was the drive? Tell me about it.'

They talked for quite a while. Then Slade strolled about the town a bit, mulling over the situation as it now stood. Looked like it was something of a stalemate. Until somebody else made one, there was no move he could make. Just have to wait and let events take their course, for the time being. Something might bust loose soon. Something was due to, sooner than he expected. When he returned to the Four Deuces he found Tobe Silvers, one of the Slash S hands, awaiting him.

'The Old Man headed for home a couple of hours back,' Tobe announced. 'Said to tell you he didn't feel right hanging around town with all that dinero on him. Garner and Fulton are with him. He said to tell you they wouldn't ride the trail through the gulch and not to worry but stay in town and have a bust with the boys.'

'Okay,' Slade replied. 'Where are the boys?'

'Oh, they're scattered all over,' answered Tobe. 'Some of 'em at the Golconda, I reckon, and at the Last Chance and the Hog Waller. I was figuring to look 'em up.'

'Go head,' Slade told him. 'I think I'll stick around here for a while.'

Some little time passed, then Hartsook came hurrying back in. For once his normally expressionless face mirrored concern.

'Slade,' he said in low tones, 'those two hellions gave me the slip. I've a notion they caught on that I was keeping tabs on them. But one of their hands told me they rode out of town about an hour ago. He said Hodson Vane was with them.'

Slade stood silently, turning the matter over in his mind. His face was bleak, his eyes cold when he spoke.

'Clyde,' he said, 'I'm going to play a hunch. There may be nothing to it, but there could be. I'm heading for the Slash S ranchhouse. Do me a favor, will you, and round up some of my boys and tell them to follow me, pronto.'

'I'll do better than that,' Hartsook replied. 'I'll grab my bunch—I know right where they all are—and ride with you.,

'That'll be fine, if you don't mind taking a risk,' Slade accepted the offer.

'I'll take a risk,' Hartsook replied grimly. 'Be right with you.'

'You'll follow me,' Slade corrected. 'I'm letting Shadow loose tonight and there's not a horse in the section that can keep up with him when he's really going strong. Come along after me as soon as you can get organized. So long!'

As he hurried to Grumley's stable, Slade admitted to himself that he was badly worried. Vane and the Masons would have no trouble gaining admittance to the ranchhouse, for Stewart had no reason to think they had evil intent. Blast it! Perhaps he should have warned old Blaine against the hellions, but he still wasn't altogether positive that he could control the rancher when he really got his bristles up. Well, he had acted for the best as he saw it. Now it was up to him to rectify the mistake, if he had made one.

It took him but a matter of minutes to secure Shadow and get the rig on him. Once clear of the town he gave the big black his head.

'Sift sand, jughead,' he told him. 'If we don't make it in time, a good man is mighty apt to die tonight, and a nice girl may wish she was dead. Trail!'

Twenty

As he raced North, Slade did some very serious thinking. He had a premonition that the whole affair was a bit too pat. What if the Bar M hand from whom Hartsook got his information had been a plant? Unwittingly so, perhaps, but set to relay the Masons' movements to the C Lazy H owner, knowing he would in turn pass the information on to him, Slade. Could be. Which would mean a trap was being set for him. Well, he'd make provisions against that.

'If we go barging up to the casa like the devil beating tanbark, we may get an unexpected and unpleasant reception,' he told Shadow. 'So we'll try a little strategy.'

As a result of his cogitations, he circled widely to the east and approached the ranchhouse from the north, halting the black while still some distance from the building.

'Stay put,' he ordered, dismounting and dropping the split reins to the ground. 'Be seeing you soon, I hope.'

With the utmost caution he stole forward on foot, approaching the house from the rear. He could see that a light burned behind shuttered windows; another in the nearest bunkhouse. Everything appeared peaceful and quiet.

Too darn peaceful and quiet, Slade felt. There was something ominous about that tense stillness, as if nature were holding its breath in apprehensive anticipation. He slowed his pace and scanned every inch of the shadowy terrain ahead. For now the huge bulk of the ranchhouse loomed close. He paused in the deep shadow beneath an old tree. His fingers fumbled with a cunningly concealed secret pocket in his broad leather belt. Another moment and the famous silver star set on a silver circle, the feared and honored badge of the Texas Rangers, gleamed on his broad chest.

For a long minute, Slade stood surveying the short stretch to the back door of the ranchhouse, which led into the kitchen and was never locked. Nowhere could he note or sense motion. It was logical to believe that the outlaws, if they really were around, would concentrate on the trail leading to the front of the house. But there was always a chance that the canny Hodson Vane would anticipate his move and have the back of the house guarded as well. However, it didn't look that way, and anyhow he had to risk it. He strode forward silently, his glance darting this way and that, and reached the back door without arousing an alarm. Slowly and with the greatest caution he turned the knob and applied a slight pressure. The door swung open easily on well-oiled hinges and he was in the kitchen. A glimmer of light seeped into the dining room from the living room beyond, and to his ears came a rumble of voices. Loosening his guns in their holsters, he slipped across the kitchen, entered the dining room and stole forward until he could see through the partly open door.

In a chair, bound hand and foot, sat old Blaine Stewart. In another chair was Ellen, her eyes great wide pools of terror. Lounging on the far side of the room were Hodson Vane and the Mason brothers, Cart and Wes.

Old Blaine was speaking and the words clearly reached Slade's ears.

'Blast you, Vane, you double-crossing skunk, you can't get away with it,' Stewart said, his voice trembling with rage. 'Slade will be after you, and he'll trail you to the gates of Hades if necessary, and shove you through them.'

'We're not worrying about Slade,' Hodson

Vane's smooth voice replied. 'He'll be taken care of—we're waiting for him to show right now. The boys will see to it that he won't aggravate us any more. Oh, he's on his way right now, charging to the rescue; we fixed it so he'd do just that. He'll be taken care of, and so will you and your two hands tied up in the bunkhouse. So that when somebody else shows up there'll be nobody around to tell what happened or to point out which way we went. Thanks, very much, for this thirty thousand; we can use it. And where you're going you won't need it. Well, guess time's about run out for you.'

Ellen gasped in her throat. Old Blaine mouthed incoherent fury. Walt Slade drew both guns. A single long stride and he was in the room. His voice rang out.

'Elevate! In the name of the State of Texas, you are under arrest! Up, I say!'

For an instant there was utter silence, broken by Ellen's glad cry. Then three pair of hands raised slowly, shoulder high. Slade's gaze, concentrating on Wes Mason's right hand, saw that hand flip forward, sliding the wicked little double-barreled .41 Derringer, the 'gambler's gun,' into his palm.

Slade shot him between the eyes. Vane's right hand whipped across his breast to his shoulder holster. Carter Mason jerked his belt gun. The room rocked and quivered to the roar of six-shooters.

204

Blood streaming down his left hand, his shirt sleeve shot to ribbons, Walt Slade peered through the smoke fog at the three motionless figures on the floor.

'Cut me loose!' bawled Stewart. 'Cut me loose! There's half a dozen more of the sidewinders in the bunkhouse, waiting for you to show! Cut me loose!'

Slade holstered his guns and bounded forward. A couple slashes of his knife freed the rancher. Outside sounded yells and the pad of running feet.

'Into the office!' Slade ordered. 'The window's barred and the door's thick. Maybe we can hold them off till Clyde and the boys get here.'

They dashed into the office, old Blaine reeling and stumbling on his numbed legs. Slade slammed the door shut and turned the key. Light from the open bunkhouse door filtered through the window to relieve the gloom.

'Lie on the floor,' Slade told Ellen. 'They'll be shooting through the window soon.'

Boots pounded the living room floor. A storm of shouts and curses arose. Something thudded against the door. Slade fired two shots through the upper panel. A wailing curse and a wild scrambling echoed the reports.

'They won't try that again,' he remarked grimly. 'I evidently winged one of them. Keep out of line with that window.'

A moment later a bullet whistled through the window and smacked against the far wall. The outlaws, grouped in front of the veranda and out of range, continued to fire. Some of the slugs, passing through the window at an angle, caromed off the hard oak wall and whined about the room.

'If we could just block that window!' Slade growled. 'One of those blasted ricochets is liable to nick somebody.'

Old Blaine was fumbling around under the big desk. 'I got something!' he exclaimed and came up with a stout wooden box. Crouching under the window, he raised it cautiously to wedge it between the frames.

'Look out!' Slade roared as a slug hit a corner of the box and knocked it from Stewart's hands. He made a frantic dive and caught the box before it slammed to the floor. Just in time the light from the bunkhouse had showed him the ominous red lettering, 'DYNAMITE.'

'Blazes! That was close!' he gasped, sweat starting out on his face. 'It's half-full of sticks. Fuse and caps, too, and it takes mighty little jar to set off a cap. If it had hit the floor we'd have all gone to glory in a basket!' He gently shoved the box into a corner.

'Now what are they up to?' he wondered. 'They've stopped shooting.'

Old Blaine was muttering and swearing. 'I forgot about that infernal stuff being in there,' he mumbled. 'Listen, I hear 'em moving around outside the door.'

Straining their ears, they could catch a slight thudding and shuffling. A moment later Ellen uttered an exclamation.

'I smell smoke!' she said.

Slade smelt it, too. From beyond the closed door came a sinister hissing and crackling.

'They've set fire to the house!' bawled Stewart. 'Guess they have,' Slade agreed. 'Looks sort of hire curtains for us.'

'Reckon the only thing we can do is charge out there and blow as many of 'em to Hades as we can before they down us,' growled Stewart.

'Yes, it looks that—' Slade began. 'Wait! That gives me a notion!'

He made a dive for the dynamite box. Swiftly he capped and fused one of the sticks, cutting the fuse perilously short. He fumbled a match from his pocket.

'Get set to jerk the door open,' he told Stewart. 'Quick, there's no time to lose!'

He touched the match to the infinitesimal length of fuse. Stewart opened the door. In the middle of the living room a heap of drapes and furniture was burning briskly. Slade bounded past it to the outer door.

The outlaws were clumped together near the foot of the veranda, watching the fire. They whooped with triumph as they sighted him. a gun cracked and a bullet whizzed past. With the fuse fire lapping the cap, Slade hurled the stick of dynamite at the group.

There was a blinding flash of yellow flame, a deafening roar. Slade was knocked back through the door and to the floor. Half stunned, he scrambled to his feet and reeled back to the door.

On the ground lay three twisted and torn bodies. The three remaining outlaws were crawling painfully away from the smoking crater the dynamite had hollowed in the ground. Slade's voice blared at them.

'Flatten out! Your hands in front of you! I'll drill the man who makes a move.'

The command was obeyed without argument. Slade was striding toward the motionless forms when from down the trail sounded a wild yelling and a clatter of hoofs. Another moment and Clyde Hartsook and his hands, with Andy Hargus and a number of the Slash S cowboys stormed into the yard. Hartsook jumped from his moving horse and ran to Slade.

'You all right?' he asked anxiously.

'Fine as frog hair,' Slade replied. 'Tie onto those hellions there, and try to put out the fire.'

The outlaws were disarmed and jerked to their feet. The cowboys rushed into the house and began throwing out the burning furniture, stamping on embers and sluicing water over the smoldering ones.

Slade approached the bound outlaws and

asked a few questions, which were answered sullenly but without hesitation. He returned to the ranchhouse, from which the smoke was clearing, and slumped wearily into a chair, while Ellen hovered over him, washing and bandaging his bullet-slashed arm.

Clyde Hartsook came in and paused in front of the ranger. 'Slade,' he asked, 'how in blazes did you figure it out?'

'Largely with your help, Clyde,' Slade replied with a smile. 'You see, I was convinced from practically the beginning that Wes Mason killed Tom Hargus. Tom was killed with a short-barreled, heavy calibre gun by somebody he had no reason to believe would do him harm, somebody able to get close enough to him to shove the gun against his ribs; and I knew Wes Mason packed that kind of a gun.'

'How's that?' Hartsook asked.

'When I got the drop on the Masons and ordered them to reach for the sky, Wes Mason's hand, after he had it up, moved forward just a trifle,' Slade explained. 'I'd seen that move before and knew what it meant. Right then Wes Mason was nearer death than he'd ever been before. If his hand had moved forward another inch to slide his sleeve gun into his palm, I'd have killed him. Later on he corroborated my deduction by not taking his coat off although he was sweating and Cart had already shucked his. At the moment I didn't know what it was all about, of course, but from the start I was puzzled at their behavior. When I requested them to examine my guns, they hardly glanced at them. Of course, they had no desire to pin Tom's killing on me. The notion was to have the Harguses blame the Stewart outfit for the killing.'

'Guess poor Tom never had a chance,' Andy Hargus interpolated sadly.

'No, he never had a chance,' Slade agreed. 'When Wes shot him, the slug knocked him from the saddle, but he managed to grab his rifle as he went down and before his horse bolted. He cut loose on the Masons with it and they hightailed into the brush. He managed to shoot off half of Wes Mason's saddle horn, which I noted. Tom staggered up the trail, turning to shoot back down it from time to time, until he dropped his rifle and later collapsed from loss of blood. When they were sure he was dead, the Masons rode to find the body. And then Wes Mason made one of the little slips the owlhoot brand always makes. He picked up Tom's fallen rifle and shoved it into his saddle boot. Cart's saddle boot was empty, and nowhere to be seen was the rifle which fired the shells I saw on the trail. I knew it must have been Tom's. Then they rode on and ran into me.'

'And trouble,' grunted Andy.

'It didn't take me long to decide that the Masons wanted Mr. Stewart killed,' Slade resumed. 'But not until I saw Cart Mason playing up to Ellen did I get any notion why. Even then I was puzzled, for the whole affair didn't seem to make sense. I was also a mite puzzled about Hodson Vane being associated with the Masons so closely, but not until you told me of his being a crooked gambler in Tombstone and an associate of such jiggers as John Ringo and his bunch did the thing begin to tie up.

'As the prisoners just told me, Vane had known the Masons in Arizona and New Mexico, where they were members of a roving owlhoot bunch. In New Mexico, they murdered a deputy sheriff. Vane knew about it and that gave him his hold on them. When he came to work for Mr. Stewart and became familiar with conditions here, he evolved his nice little scheme to get hold of the Stewart properties. He sent for the Masons and they came along, bringing some of their bunch, who kept undercover and began running cows up the trail from their land and to Mexico, partly for revenue and partly in the hope of still further embroiling the Stewart and Hargus factions, with the ultimate killing of Mr. Stewart the objective. Cart Mason, who had a way with women, was to try and catch Ellen on the rebound after her father was murdered and marry her. Later she would have met with an "accident" and Cart Mason would have inherited and Vane would have been in a position to take over, with Cart Mason as the nominal owner.'

Slade paused to roll and light a cigarette and then continued.

'It was Cart Mason who tipped Joe Callison that the Harguses were slick-ironing Slash S calves. He branded a calf and left a smoldering fire at a time he knew Tom Hargus would be riding that way, where Callison would spot him. Worked pretty well and increased the friction between the two outfits.'

'And I suppose they killed Callison?' observed Andy Hargus.

'That's right,' Slade replied. 'That was their last try at starting a real row between the outfits. When that didn't work, they set out to eliminate me and Mr. Stewart by direct methods, and came pretty near doing it. When Cart Mason overheard Clyde and me talking, they quickly figured out what I really was and decided to pull out, after grabbing Mr. Stewart's thirty thousand and his daughter. Yes, it was an ingenious scheme all around, a new wrinkle to the insurance fraud dodge—kill and collect. Hodson Vane was a man of outstanding ability and planned everything nicely. Only, it didn't work.'

'Thanks to the Texas Rangers,' Clyde Hartsook observed sententiously, with a sideways glance at old Blaine Stewart, who had sat silent the while.

'Yes, thanks to the Texas Rangers,' Stewart repeated. His gaze fixed on the gleaming silver

212

star on Slade's breast. 'And you're one of them,' he added.

'Yes, Mr. Stewart, I am one of them,' Slade said. 'I'm proud to say I'm a member of the organization you have been endeavoring to destroy, the finest and most efficient body of peace officers the world has ever known. When you resume your campaign against the rangers, Mr. Stewart, remember that a ranger saved your life. That a ranger kept your daughter from being packed off to Mexico and later murdered when that sidewinder tired of her. Remember!'

A dead silence fell over the room and all eyes were turned on Blaine Stewart, who sat staring straight ahead of him. Suddenly he raised his head and grinned, a very youthful and pleasing grin.

'Walt,' he chuckled, 'do you happen to know somebody who'd like to buy a newspaper?'

*   *   *

Muttering and mumbling under his mustache, Captain Jim McNelty spelled out an article on the front page of Blaine Stewart's *Herald*, an article that began:

When the *Herald* makes a mistake, the *Herald is* quick to admit it . . .

Captain Jim laid the paper down and

glowered at Walt Slade sitting on the opposite side of the desk, smoking comfortably.

'This thing,' he complained, 'tells all about how a ranger saved Blaine Stewart's life, cleaned out a nest of snakes and got folks together, peaceful and happy, in that blasted Alforki Valley; but it never mentions the ranger's name.'

'Guess it doesn't,' Slade agreed cheerfully.

Captain Jim pointed an accusing finger at his lieutenant. 'You wrote that article,' he said.

'Well,' Slade explained, 'Mr. Stewart insisted that I write it; he said there was nobody else around who could handle the chore as it should be handled.'

'Hrrmph!' said Captain Jim.

Slade drew a folded slip of paper from his pocket and passed it across the desk.

'What's this?' asked McNelty. Slade smiled.

'A little contribution to the fund we established to aid the dependents of rangers killed in the line of duty.'

Captain Jim's eyes widened as he read the amount of Blaine Stewart's check. Then he relieved his surcharged feelings with an explosive, 'I'll be hanged!'

We hope you have enjoyed this Large Print book. Other Chivers Press or Thorndike Press Large Print books are available at your library or directly from the publishers.

For more information about current and forthcoming titles, please call or write, without obligation, to:

Chivers Large Print
published by BBC Audiobooks Ltd
St James House, The Square
Lower Bristol Road
Bath BA2 3BH
UK
email: bbcaudiobooks@bbc.co.uk
www.bbcaudiobooks.co.uk

OR

Thorndike Press
295 Kennedy Memorial Drive
Waterville
Maine 04901
USA
www.gale.com/thorndike
www.gale.com/wheeler

All our Large Print titles are designed for easy reading, and all our books are made to last.